WHATCHA MEAN, WHAT'S A ZINE?

MARK TODD +
ESTHER
PEARL
WATSON.

→ Acknowledgments

Thanks to all the contributors, to Eden Edwards who gave us freedom to do what we wanted, "Coco" in Chatham, NY, who ~~was~~ took our zine-making workshop and showed us that there are rad 13-year-olds who zine. Thank you to Lisa Wagner-Holle and Jordan Crane for answering our annoying design questions.

Thank You to ~~&~~ Souther Salazar who helped us so much and whose typewriter I am "borrowing" to write this with. Without ~~him~~ his help many questions would stay unanswered and we would have had to hand-write even more ~~thanx~~ we did.

As you can see, the text of this book was done with a typewriter and by hand. The illustrations are done using pen, pencil, brush, copier, and whatever else we saw lying around.

www.houghtonmifflinbooks.c[om]

and have a nice day. Oh yes.

SPECIAL THANKS to CHIP ROWE[LL] FOR THE BOOK'S TITLE. Thank You

WHATCHA MEAN, WHAT'S A ZINE?

THE ART OF MAKING ZINES AND MINI COMICS

Mark Todd + Esther Pearl Watson

WITH CONTRIBUTIONS BY MORE THAN 20 CREATORS OF INDIE COMICS AND MAGAZINES.

GRAPHIA
an imprint of Houghton Mifflin Company
Boston 2006

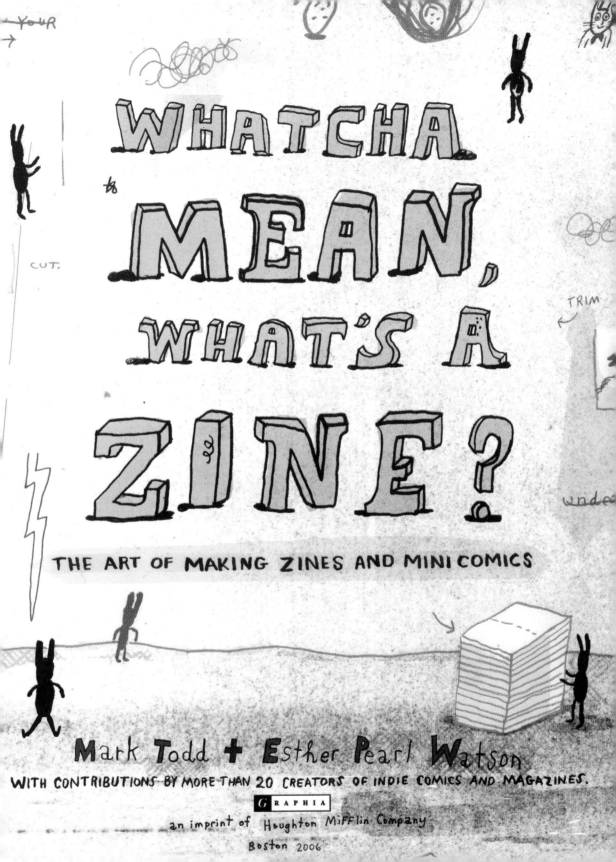

CONTENTS.

FIRST it was a zine
Now it is a magazine + stores!

0-1-1-0-0-1-1

IT'S A RACE TO THE TOP!

WS

(HELLO, I'M SMALLER)

Funky

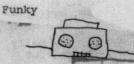

i like you.

Ditto.

YEE-HAW!

OH, IT'S ON NOW!!

power up.

HOW DO THEY MAKE IT LOOK SO EASY!?

BECAUSE THEY ROCK!

Author's Note.

We started making zines before we ever really knew what a zine was. Esther was looking at church programs, and was inspired to make ½ size sheets of paper stapled in the middle. She drew and wrote stories of lovelorn, wide-eyed teen girls. Mark's mini-comics were the superhero type, full of explosions and robots on the run. Although these handmade labors of love had cover prices and promises of follow-up issues, most were given away to friends and were short-lived.

Later, years later, we started to come across other peoples' zines. We discovered an entire world of people who created ~~their own~~ their own stories and commentary in this kind of format.

GREAT GOSH! SPY

We wanted to make a book that we would have loved to have found when we first started our mini-comics. The great thing about zines is the freedom to be able to express your thoughts any way you like. The more raw and honest, the better. It's a world where the weird, absurd, and unique is appreciated.

This book is for anyone interested in creating their own zines and learning tips and tricks from fellow zinesters.

It's for getting thoughts and ideas down on paper and into others' hands.

This book is for anyone who has something to say.

— Mark and Esther

INTRO.

Walking into a record store and scanning the bottom shelves of the diminutive magazine rack, I picked up my first zine. It was handmade using tape, typewriters, pens, and a photocopier.

It had THE ENERGY OF PUNK ROCK, but it was captured IN PRINT - all for $2. It was inspiring enough FOR ME and FRIENDS to put OUT the FIRST issue of GIANT ROBOT, A ZINE of Asian & American POP CULTURE.

THIS was in 1994. WE made a run of 240 copies and vowed to keep going.

L DRAWING

... BELOW THE RADAR of MOST, ZINES Have Gathered momentum in DIFFERENT forms. The photocopied and stapled PuBLicaTionS Filled with fun anecdotes and Comics have continued. ZineS have TAKEN on artistic STyles, many using HANDS-on TechniQues like SilkScreen, rubber stamping, PaPER FOLDING, varying Paper stocks, and DRAWING right in each Copy. Some ZineS Have No Words and are Filled with ART, PRiNTS, and PhoTography. The NUMEROUS TiTLES That you see today ARE AS iNSPiRiNG AS EVER, and HAVE LED To CAREERS.

Giant Robot has GROWN, but the MESSAGE is THE SaME. WE THINK about WHAT makes THE PROJECT FUN, Why iT is WORTHWHILE, and what makes OUR TiTLE SpeCial. The answers to THESE questions are THE Reason WhY Some people Say we're still a zine. It's also WHY ZineS WILL ConTiNuE.

ERic NaKaMuRa.

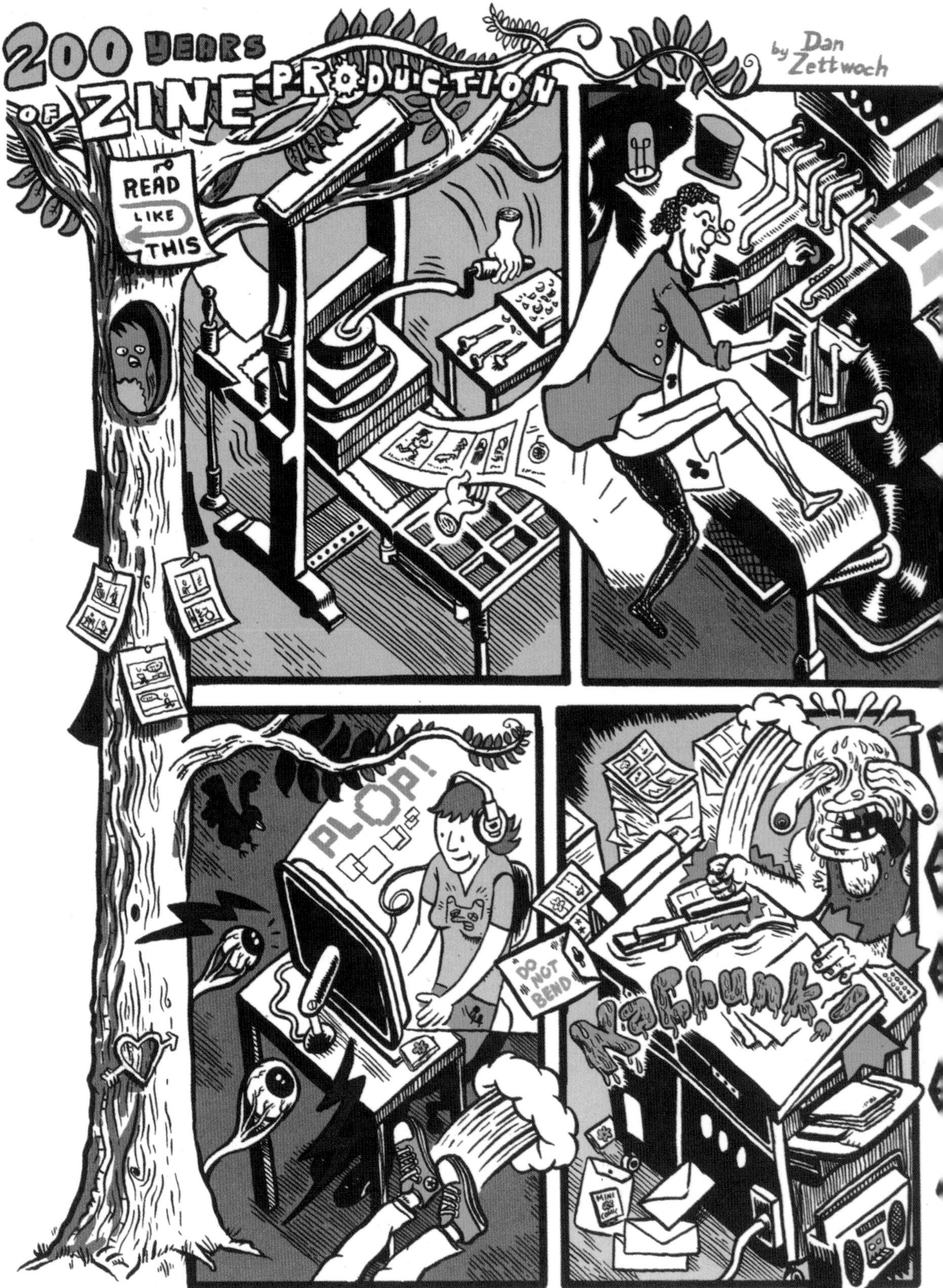
200 YEARS OF ZINE PRODUCTION
by Dan Zettwoch
READ LIKE THIS
PLOP!
DO NOT BEND
KaChunk!
MINI COMIC

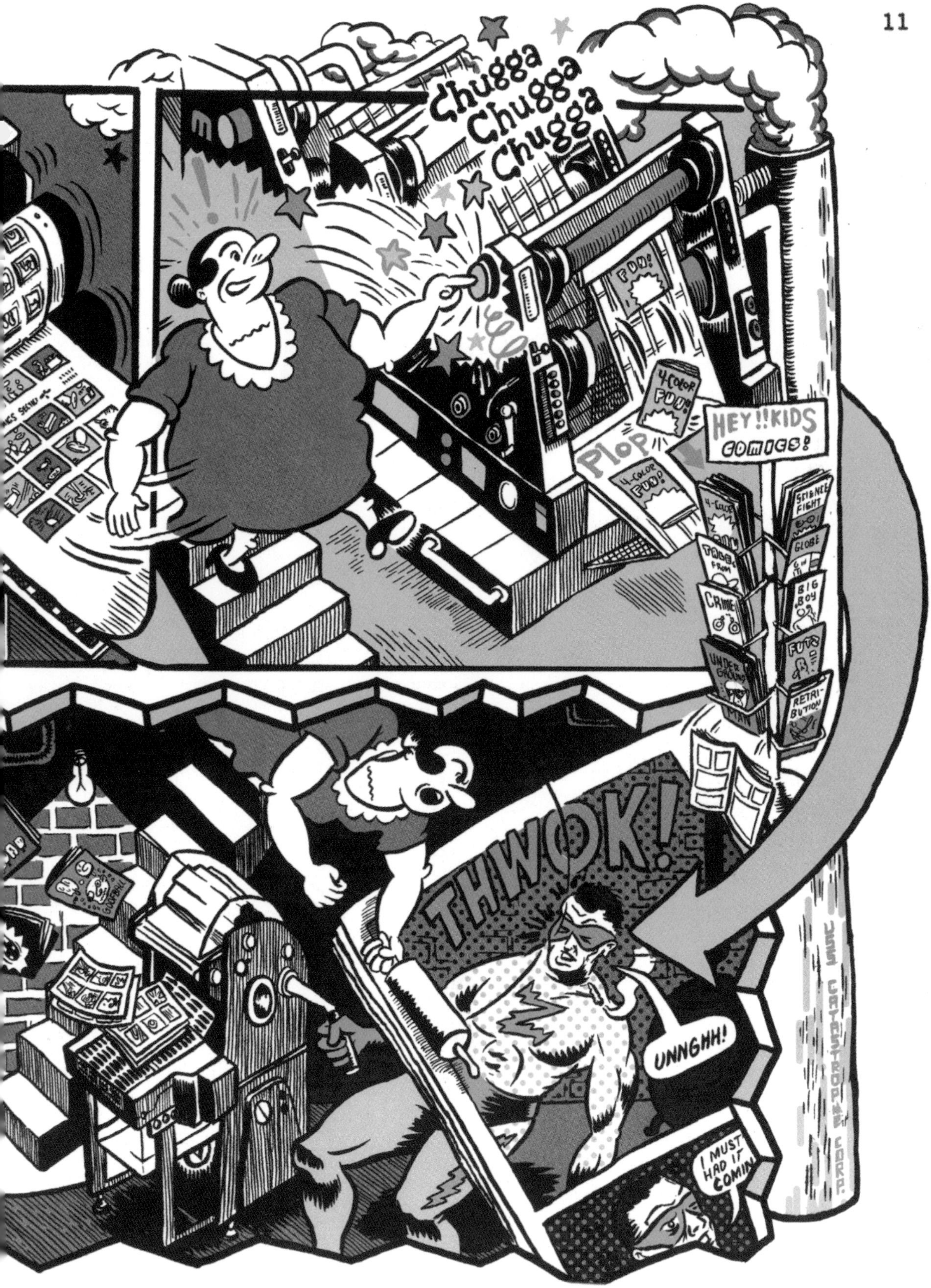
Chugga
Chugga
Chugga
4-COLOR FUN!
Plop
4-COLOR FUN!
HEY!! KIDS COMICS!
4-COLOR
TALES FROM
CRIME
UNDERGROUND MAN
SIDNEE FIGHT
GLOBE
BIG BOY
FUTZ
RETRIBUTION
THWOK!
UNNGHH!
I MUST HAD IT COMIN'
USS CATASTROPHE CORP.

WHAT'S A ZINE?

ZINES ARE CHEAPLY MADE PRINTED FORMS OF EXPRESSION ON ANY SUBJECT. THEY ARE LIKE MINI-MAGAZINES OR HOME-MADE COMIC BOOKS ABOUT FAVORITE BANDS, FUNNY STORIES, SUB-CULTURES, PERSONAL COLLECTIONS COMIX ANTHOLOGIES, DIARY ENTRIES, PATHETIC REPORT CARDS, CHAIN RESTAURANTS, AND ANYTHING ELSE.

ZINES CAN BE BY ONE PERSON OR MANY. THEY CAN BE ANY SIZE: HALF PAGE, ROLLED UP, QUARTER SIZED . . .

ZINES ARE READ BY ANYONE WILLING TO TAKE A LOOK, FROM CONCERT-GOERS and THE MAIL MAN TO PEOPLE ON THE TRAIN. THEY ARE SOLD AT BOOKSTORES, TRUMBED THROUGH AT ZINE LIBRARIES, EXCHANGED AT COMIC CONVENTIONS, and MAILED OFF TO STRANGERS.

ZINES ARE NOT A NEW IDEA. THEY HAVE BEEN AROUND UNDER DIFFERENT NAMES (CHAPBOOKS, PAMPHLETS, FLYERS). PEOPLE WITH INDEPENDENT IDEAS HAVE BEEN GETTING THEIR WORD OUT SINCE THERE WERE PRINTING PRESSES.

IT'S A GREAT FEELING TO HOLD COPIES OF YOUR ZINE IN YOUR HAND. GO AHEAD, THERE IS NO WRONG WAY.

 WHY? why? WHY?

RON REGÉ, JR.

I started making weird little mini-comics mostly because I was working at a copy shop and could make them for free. I had a P.O. Box and started to get five to ten pieces of artsy little books a week. I could take a day or two out of every month to fill orders, and create lovely packages to send to all the great people around the world.

DAVE KIERSH I've been making zines for about ten years now. I've never been a text junkie yet have picked up my fair share along the way.

ANDERS NILSEN

(a zine that reviewed other zines.)

I remember reading Factsheet Five for the first time in high school and being positively overwhelmed by the potential. It seemed like this vast world of super cool do-it-yourself culture. Zines have always been people saying what they think below the radar and flack guns of advertising dollars, political authority and social convention. Y'know, ideally.

SAELEE OH

My first zine was some crappy embarrassing thing that I made in high school and I only made about 10 copies but gave away even less than that. It probably made sense to nobody but me. I am a sucker for books with hand-made, laborious touches like silkscreened covers, collage, original drawings, stitching, etc.

JEFFREY BROWN

The great thing about zines is, because they're expected to lose money, there's no economic imperative at work, so you get a purity to the art that rarely happens elsewhere in "normal" publishing. Of course you have no editorial standards usually, so sometimes you get what you pay for.

SOUTHER SALAZAR

My brother and I started hunting down zines and mini-comics wherever we could get them. In my search I came across John Porcellino's personal stories in King-Cat Comics, which effectivly convinced me that zines might be one of the purest art forms.

WHY?

Small World Funnies BY JOHN P.

WHEN I WAS IN HIGH SCHOOL I JOINED THE SCIENCE CLUB...

CIRCA 1984

I LIKED SCIENCE ALL RIGHT, BUT MAINLY I JOINED CUZ SCIENCE CLUB WENT ON THE MOST AWESOME FIELD TRIPS...

(PLANETARIUM LASER LIGHT SHOW SYNCHRONIZED TO THE MUSIC OF PINK FLOYD)

MY FAVORITE FIELD TRIPS WERE WHEN WE WENT DOWN TO CHAMPAIGN-URBANA* FOR THE SCIENCE FAIR

SCHOOL

*HOME OF THE UNIVER-SITY OF ILLINOIS, 150 MILES FROM CHICAGO

THE SCIENCE FAIR WAS COOL, BUT AFTER LUNCH I'D SNEAK AWAY FROM THE GROUP and CHECK OUT all THE RECORD STORES and COMIC SHOPS ON GREEN STREET...

PIZZA

IT WAS MY BIG CHANCE TO FIND all THE WEIRD STUFF I WAS GETTING INTO AT THE TIME...

Adam and the Ants "PRINCE CHARMING"

ADAM & The Ants
Prince Ch.

FLaming carrot comics

Flaming Carrot ut!

ONE TIME I WAS IN RECORD SERVICE WHEN I CAME ACROSS THIS VERY STRANGE MAGAZINE

IT WAS PHOTOCOPIED, DARK, WITH all KINDS OF WEIRD ART, WRITING and POETRY

SUPER-TINY PRINT

IT WAS CALLED THE "AHTISTIC CHAINSAW GAZETTE." I DIDN'T KNOW IT AT THE TIME, BUT THIS WAS THE FIRST ZINE I EVER SAW

IT WAS AWESOME...

AFTER THAT, EVERYTIME WE WENT DOWN TO U of I, I'D LOOK FOR THE NEW ISSUE OF THE A.C.G.

READING IT ON THE BUS ON THE WAY HOME →

THIS WAS MY ENTRY WAY INTO THE WORLD OF ZINES...

TO ME, THIS STORY SUMS UP SOME OF MY FAVORITE THINGS ABOUT THE ZINE WORLD-- THAT THROUGH ZINES IT'S POSSIBLE TO COMMUNICATE WITH PEOPLE ALL OVER, and EVEN DEVELOP CLOSE FRIENDSHIPS WITH THEM-- and THAT SOMETHING AS SIMPLE AS A PHOTOCOPY CAN CHANGE SOMEBODY'S LIFE FOREVER

JOHN P. 2005 ♡
ANOTHER TRUE STORY

A PERSONAL History of ZINES

by Raina Lee
PUBLISHER OF 1-UP.

(12)

When you're a teenager and nothing appeals to you.
When nothing speaks to your experience.
When you feel like you're the only one around who thinks what
    you think and want to find others like you.

When you have something urgently, desperately, passionately
    to say, right away.
When all you have, all you can afford is a pen, paper,
    and some money for the copy machine.

When I first picked up a zine I wasn't sure x what it was, who
made it, and where it came from, but I read it cover to cover in one
sitting. It was a half-letter-sized zine with a tiny booklet in the
middle. It was covered with raw doodles and dense pages of text. The
zinex was irreverent and esoteric; I loved the fact that someone had
    thought so long and so hard about one particular thing, which ix in
this case was ways to rip off "the Man." I had nothing but respect for
the publisher to create something so few were going to read but would
at least greatly appreciate.

Hence, I became enamored with the form. I became a zine collector,
a zine publisher, and all-around zine fanatic in my teens. Zines to
me became an instantaneous paper rebellion. Anyone with a pen, paper,
and impassioned thought could make one, rich, poor, skilled, or not.
Zines are for people with something x to say, right now. Zines are
for people who don't see themselves represented in mainstream media
or x disagree about what is being said. Zines are for those who go
beyond conventional writing and opt for a melody of word and pictures,
vision and thought — cut out, glued, photocopied, and all stapled together.

While there are too many zines dead and alive to name, I can note
my own personal journey into the world of zines. I first became

interested in large format general-interest zines such as Ben Is Dead,
    and the LA-based fanzine that had started as   I Hate Brenda (of
90210 fame),a newsletter which evolved into an eclectic zine parodying other
publications and covering obscure topics. Other general interest zines

included Bunnyhop and Giant Robot, which still covers Asian and Asian
American pop culture and liestyles. Maximumrocknroll was the
    quintessential punk rockers music   zine, heavy on masculine energy and
holier-than-thoughpunk attitude, and Punk Planet (which is still in print)

                        covers music from a

politicized and community oriented viewpoint.

Zines are also hard to find since you can't find them at your nearest chain bookstore;to be keyed into the zine community check out review zines, where people send in their work to be honestly reviewed. The biggest and most widely read review zine was Factsheet Five, which is now defunct. FF5 had, in addition to reviews, updated addresses and underground publishing news.

Another genre is that of the thematic fanzine, which focused on a very specific subject matter almost to the point of exhaustion. Early fanzines on science fiction fantasy proliferated in the 1950s . Some even argue that Thomas Paine's 1776 Common Sense was a zine. Zines as we know them xxxxx started mostly as fanzines about bands and politics in the 80 s.

What I really appreciate,however,are zines on esoteric subjects - the strange, the trivial, and the obscure. A zine called The Palindromist was entirely about, um, palindromes, Beer Frame reviewed strange consumer products such as sauerkraut juice. Duplex xx Planet published by a nursing home worker compiled interviews of older folks and their wise and comical views of life. A favorite zine of mine was Scaredy Cat Stalker, a hilarious pub devoted to fxxx fearful "stalking" of E.T. child star Henry Thomas. Stalker parodied the traditional zealous star-zine by being zealous but sarcastically mocking of its object of desire.

Another zine was entirely about making milk crate furniture.

The most common kind of zine is the personal zine, created by individuals reflecting on their everyday lives - confessional, sometimes mundane, containing even scandalous writings.

The most well known personal zine, which is still in publication, is Cometbus, published by an older punk rocker in Berkeley, California. Cometbus's endearing reflections about his travels is a kind of diary of the punk rock life: traveling, seeing bands, and visiting friends. What always amazes me about Cometbus is that the text-dense zine is entirely handwritten in uppercase; no typewriter or word processor here. Doris is like a female Cometbus about a woman who suffers from depression. Her writings and observations tend to make her readers want to hug her and cry.

Personally, I was inspired by the zines that came out of Riot Grrrl ███, a movement that incited young women to start bands, make art and create zines about their experiences. I was compelled by zines that xix critiqued mainstream representations of gender and race. I'm So Fxxxing Beautiful, which dealt with female body issues and representations of normative beauty, and Tennis and Violins and Slander, which both focused on queer Asian feminist politics. Evolution of a Race Riot, edited by Mimi Nguyen, collected writings by queer, women, and people, of color in punk rock, critiquing racism and sexism within that scene. I started to publish my own zine on feminist writings that mixed fragmented thoughts, essays, and cut-out graphics.

Through zining I've met dozens of other zinesters, many of whom have become my closest and dearest friends. By ordering zines reviewed in Giant Robot I met my dear friend Scott from his zine Yob. I've gotten dates from zines, too, an untold perk. Zines have changed my life, and given me confidence to know that I can say whatever I want, print it, and leave it in the world, so someone can read it and possibly understand.

Zines tend to have a short lifespan and sporadic publishing schedules based on the whim of the publisher. The ephemeral quality of zine publishing and the form itself make zines precious but fleeting objects. Most zinesters stop publishing after a year or two, with exceptions being Cometbus, and popular zines that grow and become magazines such as Bust, Giant Robot, XLR8R, and Dazed and Confused. However, a few vibrant new zines are being published today, including the irrepressible Found Magazine which collects "found" and jettisoned objects, photographs, letters, and other curiosities. Cheap Date is a trashy but humorous fashion zine. Drunken Master and Pencil Fight are combinations of illustrative artwork, writing, and interviews. I currently publish 1-UP which collects personal writing and artwork related to video game culture. Often people who have never "zined" ask why I choose to print instead of publish online: I state that it's obvious-how will we remember websites 5 years or even 20 years from now? I have more faith xi in zines as a unique tangible expression, a photocopied thought that someone could hold, pass to someone at a show, and find (again and again) at the bottom of your underwear drawer.

The Evolution of Self-Publishing.

1950s Allen Ginsberg, Jack Kerouac, and other Beat Poets publish chapbooks.

1950 Xerox Corporation makes photocopy machine commercially available.

1970 Kinkos Opens in Santa Barbara, Ca.

1976 Sniffin' Glue Early punk zine started by Mark Perry.

1937 Process called Xerography invented by Chester Carlson.

1977 Riso launches silkscreen toy printer "Print Gocco B6 ." Zinsters see zine cover potential.

1930 The Comet , early sci-fi fanzine published by the sci-fi correspondence club.

1982 Maximumrockandroll, radio show turns zine.

1982 " Factsheet 5 , a zine that reviews zines, started by Mike Gunderloy.

1923 Wilhelm Ritzerfeld invents ditto Ditto Machine.

1984 Apple introduces the first Mac.

1985 First "desktop publishing" application (Page Maker) by Aldus.

1907 Samuel Simon of England patents process of using silk fabric as a printing screen.

1988 Hewlett Packard's DeskJet inkjet printer at competative price.

1989 Epson releases single-pass color flatbed scanner.

1888 Albert Blake Dick improves mimeograph process.

Early 1990s Time Warner produces the zine Dirt , inspired by underground zine world.

1879 George W. Mc Gils patents Single-Stroke Stapler.

1991 Allison Wolte and Molly Neuman publish Riot Grrrl zine.

1872 Lebbeus H Rogers saw potential for making copies of office documents with carbon paper.

1829 William Austin Burt patents axmaxhime typewriter.

2000s E-zines explosion:the web increases availability and information across the globe.

GAME BOY

ZINE

START

GREAT MOMENTS in ZINE HISTORY

BY JOE ROCCO

① IN 1733 BENJAMIN FRANKLIN SELF-PUBLISHED "POOR RICHARD'S ALMANAC"... LATER THAT YEAR, HE CREATED THE FIRST "HOT LIST" FOR PEOPLE MAGAZINE

HMMM... BETSY ROSS... TOTALLY HOT!

INK

② HOW FABULOUS IS THAT?

HA!

William Blake

ARTIST, POET AND CHRONIC BED-WETTER WILLIAM BLAKE GRADUALLY PERFECTED ENGRAVING TECHNIQUES FROM THE LATE 1700S THROUGH THE EARLY 1800S UNTIL HIS DEATH IN 1827.

③

·CLICK!

PLEASE BUY MY AMWAY PRODUCTS ...HELLO...STILL THERE?

THOMAS EDISON INVENTED THE MIMEOGRAPH OR "STENCIL DUPLICATOR" IN 1875. IT WAS THE PREDECESSOR TO THE MODERN PHOTOCOPIER, BUT RELIED ON SPECIAL STENCILS.

④ SAMIZDAT (TRANSLATED FROM THE RUSSIAN "SAM", MEANING "SELF" AND "IZDATELSTVO", MEANING "PUBLISHING") WAS A MOVEMENT IN POST-STALINIST RUSSIA. BEFORE GLASNOST IN THE 1980S IT WAS THE ONLY WAY TO PUBLISH ANYTHING WITHOUT CENSORSHIP.

UGLY NAGGING WIFE SHE DRIVE ME TO SELF-PUBLISH.

IS JOKE NO?

EVERYBODY IS COMEDIAN.

DAVE KIERSH

PIONEERS & STAMP LICKERS

1 THE LATE 1930s: ROBERT LOWRY PUBLISHES THE LITTLE MAN MAGAZINE WHILE IN HIS FIRST YEAR OF COLLEGE. WITH THE PROFITS HE BUYS HIS OWN PRINTING PRESS AND BEGINS PUBLISHING SMALL LITERARY PAMPHLETS WITH ARTIST JIM FLORA, SOMETIMES IN EDITIONS AS SMALL AS ONLY ONE HUNDRED COPIES.

2 IN THE EARLY 1950s RAY JOHNSON BEGAN DESTROYING MOST OF HIS PAINTINGS, CUTTING THEM UP AND USING THEM ALONG WITH PARTS OF COMICS & MAGAZINES TO MAKE COLLAGED POSTCARDS.

3 THROUGHOUT THE MID-1960s: AN AMATEUR SUPER-HERO COMIC BOOK WAS PUBLISHED BY THREE TEXANS. STAR-STUDDED COMICS RAN FOR 18 ISSUES & FEATURED THE FAN FAVORITE XAL-KOR, THE HUMAN CAT, CREATED BY A YOUNG RICHARD GREEN. "GRASS-GREEN WOULD BECOME ONE OF THE MOST HIGHLY REGARDED AFRICAN-AMERICAN CARTOONISTS OF THE 1970s.

4 BY THE EARLY 1980s, BRADLEY JOHNSON BEGAN PRODUCING HIS MINI-COMIC "ITCHY & SCALY." HIS IRREVERENT HUMOR, WACKY CHARACTERS AND UNIQUE DRAWING STYLE WOULD BE SEEN IN VARIOUS ZINES AND UNDERGROUND COMIX FOR THE FOLLOWING 20 YEARS.

5 BY THE MID 1990s: JOHN PORCELLINO'S "SPIT AND A HALF" CATALOG WAS IN FULL SWING. THIS MAIL ORDER CATALOG FEATURED NEARLY A HUNDRED ZINES & MINI-COMICS. IT WAS INSTRUMENTAL IN CREATING A PRE-INTERNET NETWORK AMONGST NEW CREATORS.

FROM A ZINE to MAGAZINE.

an Interview with Laurie Henzel co-Founder of BUST magazine.

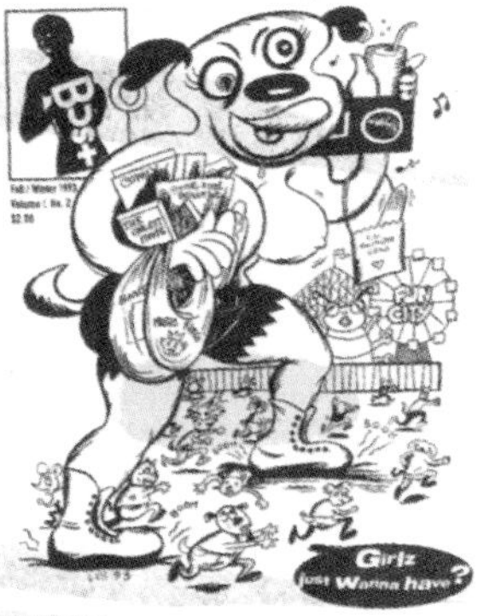
Girlz
just Wanna have?

1st Bust Zine: 500 copies

Bust Magazine: circulation 81,000

How did BUST get started?

– My friends Debbie Stoller, Marcelle Karp, and I were working at Nickelodeon in 1993. I was a designer there, slapping logos on stationery. Debbie and Marcelle came up with the idea to create a cool zine for women. They Xeroxed and stapled this thing in the office at night. People liked it so they asked me to help on the second issue because they needed a designer

If all three of you had day jobs, when did you work on BUST?

→ We would work on nights and weekends.

How was putting BUST together with friends?

For the most part, it was really fun and exciting, especially seeing the finished product.

→ How did you start distributing BUST?

We brought it around to a couple of stores. There was a store called SEE HERE in the East Village. They liked it and started selling them for us.

So, the first issue of BUST was created on a copy machine—what about the other early issues?

For the second issue we found this printer in Queens who printed it for us on newsprint. The cover was 2 color, pink and black with a cartoon by Lynn Von Schlicting. The third issue looked terrible on the newsprint, way too dark, but we learned as we went along.

When did you first start taking subscriptions?

We didn't officially ask for subscriptions till issue four (Summer/Fall of 1994.) I guess it took us a year to figure out that we would keep going for a while.

Was Thurston Moore the first big interview?

No, in Issue 5 (winter/Spring 95) we interviewed Ann Magnuson, and lots of bands, like Veruca Salt and Lucious Jackson. But Thurston was the first time we ever put a "personality" on the cover. Before that they were only concept covers.

Advice for getting + interviewing well-known musicians?

It's hard to get really famous bands, but you can always try hanging out after a show to ask! No stalking! Or if he band is small enough, call or e-mail the label and ask them. Most bands are happy for the publicity when they are starting out. The music industry has always supported zines.

Okay, thanks!

A SHORT LIST OF PEOPLE INTERVIEWED IN BUST,

BJÖRK
COURTNEY LOVE.
MARGARET CHO
JANEANE GAROFALO
LILI TAYLOR, BECK
PJ HARVEY,
GLORIA STEINEM
JOSH HOMME, CHER,
RUFUS WAINWRIGHT.
FRANCES McDORMAND
YOKO ONO,
CHRISSIE HYNDE. +
(A COVER BY
RITA ACKERMAN.)

a drawing of Laurie Henzel from memory

THE CHALLENGE: WRITE, DRAW & PUBLISH A MINICOMIC
BY shane patrick boyle

Sometimes, as a creative exercise, some of my friends and I participate in a challenge to write, draw and publish a minicomic by a specified deadline

I'm participating in such a challenge right now. And I'm actually the one who issued the challenge, so I'm sort of obligated to have a comic finished by... uh tomorrow

AND LOOK AT THE TIME*

*I don't really wear a watch

At this point, I'm having doubts about my abilities and having trouble coming up with ideas, but I have a deadline so I have to come up with....

SOME THING

I can't draw (And to be honest, my writing is a bit rusty too)

And my penmanship is really awful

And the whole thing is going to be a Rush Job

THS COMIC IS going to SUCK

Photo Copier

fold

staple

BUT...

I Have to Keep going

I can't let any of these facts stop me from

MY COMIC

FINISHING

Meat 'N' Potatoes.

So, what's it gonna be? Pull up a chair, put your feet on the table and let your mind wander. Topics could be about anything, as important as the meaning of life, or as dull as the insoles of your shoes.

Making lists is a good start. List the places you have lived, the people you have met at the copystore, meals you have shared with others, neighbors, bad movies to laugh at. what about that annoyingly itchy tag on the back of your shirt?

You don't have to be an artist. Use collage elements to dress up the look of your zine. You don't have to draw the art yourself, you can work with someone who loves to draw. Co-op! It doesn't matter if you are all words or all art, you just have to have a voice, an attitude and something to say!

(Access to a copy machine and a long-arm stapler wouldn't hurt either.)

Can't start?

Afraid you won't finish? Then zine about never being able to finish. Think no one would be interested in what you have to say? Zine for yourself! Letting go of your fears may help you break free of creative blocks. Break larger goals down into little ones. It builds confidence to accomplish smaller projects like a four-page zine instead of a sixty-four-page one. It also helps to tune out the critic inside your head while you're working.

Every time you make a new zine, you get better, faster, learn tricks.

How do you become inspired?
Collect zines you like.
Look at places that no one
else looks for ideas.
Look at what is around
you for ideas.

> KEEP your eyes
> and ears open.
> Look up - Look down -
> Look around.

zine about

CHALLENGE YOURSELF

Sometimes it's the process of zine making that is the art, not the finished product. Enjoy the struggle and accidents that occur.

Don't be afraid to take on a task too big. You can make disposable zines as warm -ups.

Do something out of character.
Do something that makes you say, "I'm going to regret this!"

Find a way to work flaws into your art. Come up with unique copy machine tricks with that crappy machine you're forced to use.

ON WHALING

A HOW-TO BY ANDERS NILSEN

I WOULD SAY THAT THE QUESTION I GET ASKED THE MOST IS "WHERE DO YOU GET YOUR IDEAS?"

... ACTUALLY I'M NOT SURE I'VE EVER BEEN ASKED THAT.

BUT ANYWAYS, MY ANSWER IS ALWAYS THE SAME: DIVINE INSPIRATION

GOD TELLS ME ALL MY IDEAS.

WHICH I GUESS TECHNICALLY MEANS THEY'RE NOT MINE.

THERE MAY BE A LAWSUIT.

BUT ANYWAYS, IF YOU ARE NOT THAT LUCKY, TO GET YOUR IDEAS FROM THE LORD, I HAVE SOME OTHER SUGGESTIONS.

BUT FIRST SOME PITFALLS AND A FEW TOPICS TO MAKE SURE AND AVOID.

1. DON'T FOMENT RESISTANCE TO THE EXISTING SOCIAL ORDER. THIS HAS BEEN DONE A MILLION TIMES, IT'S OLD HAT, AND WHILE FUN AND VITALLY IMPORTANT, IT COULD BE DANGEROUS TO YOUR HEALTH, JUST ASK FRED HAMPTON.

DO NOT WRITE DOWN YOUR PSYCHO-SPIRITUAL SURVIVALIST MASTER PLAN FOR THE END OF THE WORLD. SOCIETY IS NOT READY FOR THIS YET. WAIT A YEAR OR SO, UNTIL THINGS HAVE REALLY GONE TO HELL.

3. YOUR FAVORITE BAND. I WON'T PROHIBIT THIS ONE OUTRIGHT, BECAUSE I KNOW IT WILL DO NO GOOD, HOWEVER I WILL PLEAD WITH YOU TO BE CAREFUL, BE SURE YOU ARE EMOTIONALLY READY, TALK IT OVER WITH YOUR PARTNER BEFORE HAND, AND ABOVE ALL— USE PROTECTION!

ONE SURE-FIRE USEFUL TRICK TO GETTING GOOD IDEAS IS TO ACCUMULATE DIVERSE EXPERIENCES AND LIVE AN INTERESTING LIFE. I HAVE NOT TRIED THIS MYSELF, IT SEEMS DANGEROUS. BUT I KNOW THAT HERMAN MELVILLE AND ERNEST HEMING-WAY GOT A LOT OF MATERIAL THIS WAY FOR THEIR ZINES ABOUT WHALING.

ANOTHER GOOD STRATEGY IS TO INTERVIEW MEMBERS OF THE COMMUNITY ABOUT CURRENT EVENTS. YOU COULD ASK THE ▮▮▮▮ BARBER ABOUT TRENDS IN FOOTWEAR, OR THE OLD LADY ACROSS THE STREET WHAT SHE THINKS ABOUT GLOBAL WARMING.

LASTLY YOU CAN ALSO JUST STEAL IDEAS. THIS IS ACTUALLY VERY PRACTICAL. YOU CAN JUST LEAN OVER AND LOOK AT YOUR NEIGHBOR'S PAPER, OR ELSE GET ONE OF THESE BRAIN SCANNING ▮▮▮▮ MIND READER HELMETS FROM THE SHARPER IMAGE CATALOG.

IF NONE OF THESE WORK FOR YOU, AND YOU CAN'T AFFORD THE HELMET, HERE ARE SOME GUIDELINES THAT ARE SURE TO YIELD PRODUCTIVE RESULTS. AND NOW I'M BEING SERIOUS.

GOD STARTED TALKING TO ME WHEN I DID THIS.

 FIRST, YOU NEED A CLOCK.

 THEN: GET A NOTEBOOK OR ABOUT 40 to 60 pieces OF PAPER. DRAW ONE ~~ANIMAL~~ OF THREE THINGS, AN ANIMAL, A ROBOT, OR YOUR MOM'S BOYFRIEND.

MAKE IT VERY SIMPLE.

STICK FIGURES ARE FINE.

 OKAY, NOW YOU HAVE 60 SECONDS TO ~~█~~ THINK OF SOMETHING ~~█████~~ FOR IT TO SAY OR DO.

WHEN SIXTY SECONDS IS UP YOU HAVE TO TURN THE PAGE AND START ON THE NEXT ONE.

THE NEXT ONE IS THE NEXT PANEL, AND YOU ONLY HAVE 60 SECONDS TO DRAW IT, SO THINK FAST.

 IF YOU CAN'T THINK OF SOMETHING FOR ONE PANEL, THAT'S OKAY. IT'S JUST A PAUSE IN THE ACTION.

 IN COMICS PAUSES ARE LIKE ANVILS: THEY CONTRIBUTE A SENSE OF GRAVITY.

YOU CHANGE EVERY 60 SECONDS FOR AN HOUR. WHEN YOU ARE DONE YOU WILL BE SURPRISED.

YOU WILL HAVE STARTER MATERIAL FOR YOUR NEXT **10** MINI-COMICS.

WHAT'S THE BIG IDEA?

Here's a list of things you could make a zine about,

TREASURE HUNT. Make a list and let the readers hunt! Hide the clues all over town...in the bathroom stall of a certain chain store, on a park bench, in a phone booth...

DETOUR. Things to avoid at all costs.

MY PARENTS' VINYL COLLECTION. Music Music your parents own...a sampling of their strangeness. Devote a page or two to psycho-analyzing their taste.

ESCAPED FROM THE NUT HOUSE. Describe a person you know who drives you crazy.

DEAR DIARY. Celebrate the ordinary in your life, be careful to highlight the most mundane so that others find multiple meaning in nothing!

XXXXXXXXXXX
DIARY DINNER

FOUND GARBAGE. Reproduce papers you find in the garbage, at school, at work, on the subway, on the sidewalk...

DETOUR Things to avoid at all costs

EAR PLUGS PLX PLEASE. A little meditation on the lyrics of the worst song ever created.

SHOPPING FINDS. Good at finding treasures for dirt cheap? Detail your adventures, reveal your secrets, pass along some helpful tips!

BE USELESS. Create a how-to guide for those who would rather sleep in and not participate in anything of worth or value.

ANARCHIST BIBLE. Preach to dark side the many waves of punk; the beauty in ignoring rules, chores, and other orderly behaviors.

BLACKMAIL. Start a collection of things said, embarrassing moments, secret photos, diary pages, and print them to sway things your way.

OLD SCHOOL. Illustrate your best web log moments (or better yet, someone else's) and and put it into print for posterity.

RESTRAINING ORDER. Describe an obsession. Make sure to repeat yourself over and over and over...Use the word LOVE a lot. This helps make your point and convince the reader you are over the edge.

YEARBOOK. Go through your yearbook and tell what you remember about each person.

MINI MANIFESTO. Make a list of offenses in an area you believe strongly in...from conditions of animals kept in zoos to foul play in take-out menu design.

MASS TRANSPORTATION. Detail the daily grind of mass transportation.

A YARD SALE ZINE. Chop up everything you own and bind it. ONe man's belongings are another man's reading material.

PUBLIC SIGNS. Collect signs from public places. and make

LOST & FOUND. Photocopy notices stapled to telephone poles or
in public bathrooms reminding the public to use toilet etiquette.

BLOCK PARTY. Collect notes, drawings, writings, rumors,
anything really, from people who live on your block.

IDIOT. Describe the most embarassing moments of your life or have
each of your friends describe something really moronic that
happened to them.

BAD POETRY. Collect overly sentimental or way-too-angry poems from
the unsuspecting.

SCHOOL NOTES. Photocopy your fine collection of confiscated notes
found in classrooms, school bathrooms, empty lockers, on campus...

BOOK OF RULES. Make a list of absurd (or logical) rules you believe
people should adapt into their daily lives. It's common sense people...

PET DIARY. Make a list of everything your pooch does every 10 minutes:
11:09 a.m. sleep, 11:19 sleep, 11:29 a.m. snoring slightly...

So ANNOYING. These are those things that bug the nerves right
out of your skin. There simply isn't enough paper in the world
to list them all...

TAKE IT TO THE STREET. Take photos documenting a journey from A to B:
curbs, stairs, rails, mailboxes, brick walls, chainlink fences...

MASS CONSUMPTION. Detail your experience in the world of franchises,
trend followers, useless technology, and constant barrages of advertisements

INTERVIEWS. Write up your list of questions and then attack! We all
want to hear a conversation between you and
your gaming brother, or the old lady in the nursing home, or your fast-food
employer, or that graffiti guy.

PURE GENIUS. This is a little ditty about a genius who no one has
heard of but everyone should know. It's about time!

EVERYONE LOVES A CRITIC. Make a review zine. review examples: cps other zines, books, etc.
Give the title, list the artists, writers,
and what it's about.
I DON'T Describe or show what it looks like and provide any commentaries you have.

WHY? WHY NOT?

having fun with

MATERIALS

TIPS#TRICKS*POINTERS (in some kind of order-maybe)

by souther

OUR MOTTO: →

go crazy!!

INSTRUCTIONS

When it comes to making zines, there's no one-stop shop for materials. But you're in luck; good junk is all around you! The enterprising young zinester must find ~~them~~ her tools of the trade wherever & whenever she can -- rubbing shoulders with such unlikely colleagues as businessmen (in office supply stores) and old ladies (in scrapbook/craft supply stores) to find that special something that'll make the next zine just right. ANYTHING CAN GO INTO THE MIX. Sometimes a good zine starts with a found material that ~~can~~ inspires content to follow→

(for example)

ONE DAY:

HEY! A SHOELACE!

THE NEXT DAY:

THE MISSING SHOE-LACE

ANYWAYS -- here's some stuff to remember: KEEP AN EYE OUT -- ALWAYS BE LOOKING. YARD SALES, FLEA MARKETS, GARBAGE PILES, ETC. OFFICE SUPPLY STORES going-out-of-business-sales are the jackpot. THINK IN MULTIPLES: when you find a bunch of something cool -- think, "how can i make a zine with these??" KEEP IT CHEAP -- free is good. you can pass the savings on when you rescue discarded things, and help save the planet. KEEP IT REAL: when you're done getting all fancy-schmancy, remember -- all you really need is A PEN, SOME PAPER, AND A LOT OF HEART.

WHAT COULD YOU DO WITH THESE???

GOOD LUCK!

ONCE YOU'VE GATHERED ENOUGH STUFF, SET UP SHOP!

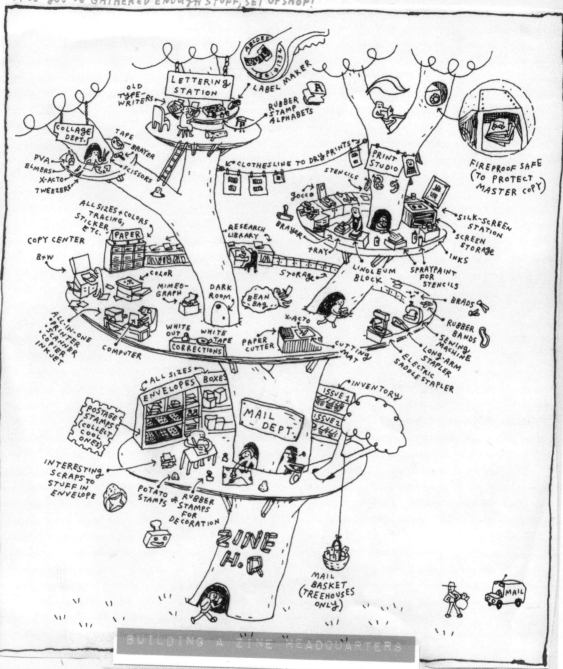

BUILDING A ZINE HEADQUARTERS

MY FIRST ZINE HEADQUARTERS WAS IN AN UNUSED OFFICE ABOVE MY DAD'S ANTIQUE STORE. ME AND MY BROTHER HATCHED ALL KINDS OF PLANS UP THERE AND MADE A COOL BLOWN UP XEROX POSTER FOR THE DOOR THAT SAID "JUNK HQ." (JUNK WAS OUR ZINE) WE KEPT ALL OUR MASTER COPIES IN AN OLD SAFE THAT SOMEONE LEFT BEHIND.

WRITING

BETWEEN MT. FUJI AND MT. SAINT HELENS.

BY Christopher Lepkowski

In Peter Bagge's comic book Hate, the character Buddy Bradley yells, "I'd rather put out a zine about **rocks** than about 'rock'!" And you could, you know. You could do a zine about rocks, or pebbles, or little pieces of dirt. Chunks of asphalt. Boulders. Mountains. Mountains!

But at some point, while you're laying out pictures of all the peaks you've visited, you'll probably want to put some writing in there. Just for filler. To cover that blank area between Mt. Fuji and Mt. Saint Helens.

◆ No one can tell you what to write, but here's a short list to get you thinking:

RANTS

You can write about how much you love something or how much you can't stand it. You can present a manifesto of your beliefs about love or God or politics or what school is really about or what family is really about. You can whisper your questions and scream your answers (or vice-versa).

Fiction

A lot of options here. Make up a story and present it all at once or in installments in each issue. You can do group fiction where each of your buddies writes one page and then passes it on. Or even do a group story all in one evening, sitting around the kitchen table with Mountain Dews in hand and the radio on, passing the page around sentence by sentence till it's done.

POETRY

The danger zone. Poetry's so great (in theory), but so much of it is bad. Oh, I'm sure yours will be good, all about how you felt while curling your way up the cliff face to the top of that mountain in Appalachia.

DIARY/JOURNAL

There's no better way to share your thoughts than to quit writing "Dear Diary" and instead write to the rest of us. The zine <u>Burn Collector</u> by Al Burian is mostly made up of description of his own life: where he lives, what he's been doing, and how he's been feeling, and it's great! Sad and funny--that's the hallmark of really good writing and the stamp of "real life" in general.

REVIEWS

Give your opinions on books, comics, records, movies or anything else--we all need help finding the good stuff and weeding out the bad. You're doing the community a ~~xxxxxx~~ service, you know you are.

NONFICTION/ARTICLES

Maybe you know an ungodly amount of some obscure knowledge--SAY, the techniques and equipment needed to construct a collapsible top hat. Or maybe you're fascinated by the film work of singer Dolly Parton and wonder why you've never seen a thorough investigation of her development as an actor, from ~~9 to 5~~ <u>9 to 5</u> to <u>The Best Little Whorehouse in Texas</u> to <u>Rhinestone</u> and so on and on. Write about it! Why not?

People's brains are aching to be filled and there's no topic that can't be made interesting.

INTERVIEWS

If you really don't feel like making up all that talk, talk, talk by yourself, you can do interviews. They're a good way to make your readers feel like they've gotten to sit down with someone and learn about them. (Of course that's an illusion--you got the best part, you actually got to do the sitting and chatting.)

The Daily News.

Whether or not you keep a journal tucked away under your mattress or online for all to see, zines are a great way to get it down and out.

Here are some inspirational ideas to write about daily... perhaps something a bit juicier than what you ate for lunch.

1) **Write and/or draw** for ten minutes without stopping...whatever comes to mind.

2) **Make a list of a taste, touch smell, sight,** or. **sound.**

3) **Finish the sentence:**
Today i saw _____,
it reminded me of _____,
and i felt _____.

4) Write **about someone else, a different person each day. An overheard conversation, someone you saw outside the window. What do they want? What do they think they want? What are they struggling against? Create a list of questions to answer for them.**

under you

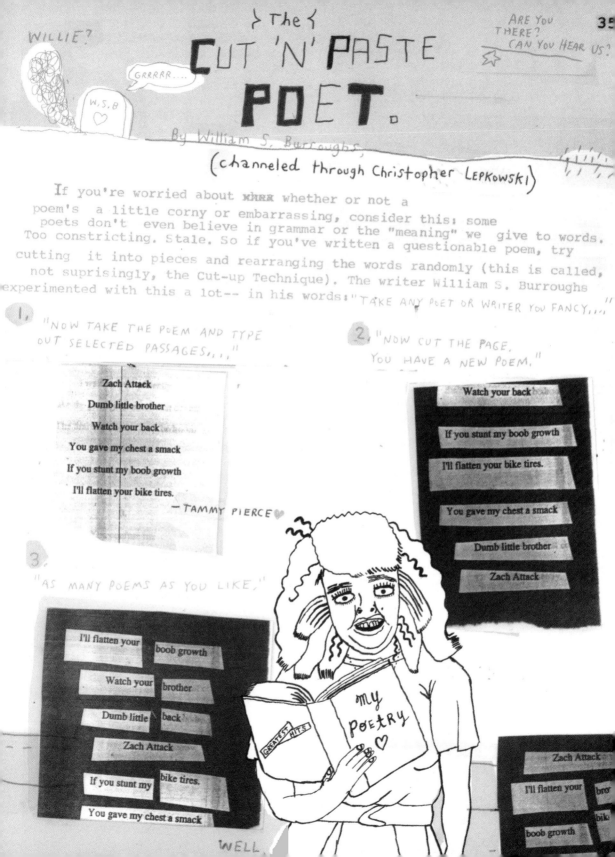

The CUT 'N' PASTE POET.

By William S. Burroughs

(channeled through Christopher Lepkowski)

WILLIE?

GRRRRR....

W.S.B ♥

ARE YOU THERE? CAN YOU HEAR US?

If you're worried about ~~whxx~~ whether or not a poem's a little corny or embarrassing, consider this: some poets don't even believe in grammar or the "meaning" we give to words. Too constricting. Stale. So if you've written a questionable poem, try cutting it into pieces and rearranging the words randomly (this is called, not surprisingly, the Cut-up Technique). The writer William S. Burroughs experimented with this a lot-- in his words: "TAKE ANY POET OR WRITER YOU FANCY,,,,"

1. "NOW TAKE THE POEM AND TYPE OUT SELECTED PASSAGES,,,,"

Zach Attack

Dumb little brother

Watch your back

You gave my chest a smack

If you stunt my boob growth

I'll flatten your bike tires.

— TAMMY PIERCE ♥

2. "NOW CUT THE PAGE, YOU HAVE A NEW POEM."

Watch your back
If you stunt my boob growth
I'll flatten your bike tires.
You gave my chest a smack
Dumb little brother
Zach Attack

3. "AS MANY POEMS AS YOU LIKE,"

I'll flatten your   boob growth
Watch your   brother
Dumb little   back
Zach Attack
If you stunt my   bike tires.
You gave my chest a smack

my POETRY ♥

GREATEST HITS

Zach Attack
I'll flatten your   bro
bike.
boob growth

WELL

THE ART OF THE INTERVIEW

IF THE EYES ARE THE WINDOW TO THE SOUL THEN THE SOUND OF THE TONGUE AGAINST THE SOFT PALETTE IS THE LAUNDRY CHUTE. AUTOGRAPHS ARE FOR AMATEURS: SAVVY INDIVIDUALS INTERVIEW THEIR HEROES.

THE TRUTH ABOUT CELEBRITIES

THE SECRET ABOUT FAMOUS PEOPLE IS THEY MOSTLY LIKE TO BE INTERVIEWED, THAT'S PART OF WHAT MAKES THEM FAMOUS. WOULDN'T YOU BE EXCITED IF SOMEONE WANTED TO INTERVIEW YOU? IT'S USUALLY NOT AS HARD TO SET UP AN INTERVIEW AS YOU MIGHT THINK. IF YOU'RE INTERVIEWING THEM IN PERSON YOU CAN USE A WALKMAN WITH A BUILT-IN MICROPHONE, IF IT'S OVER THE PHONE, THERE ARE ADAPTORS WHICH PLUG INTO THE CORD SO YOU CAN TAPE IT.

(MAKE SURE YOU ASK FIRST).

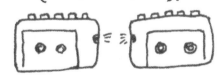

TO DO THE BRAINSTORMING AND PREPARING. ALSO IF YOU'RE GOING TO ASK ANYTHING THAT MIGHT POTENTIALLY PISS OFF THE PERSON YOU'RE INTERVIEWING SAVE THOSE QUESTIONS FOR LAST.

TRANSCRIBING

THIS IS WAY TIME-CONSUMING BUT ALSO KIND OF FASCINATING TO LISTEN TO THE ECCENTRICITIES OF HUMAN SPEECH PATTERNS AIDED BY THE HYPER AWARENESS THAT COMES FROM WRITING OUT EVERY WORD. FOR ME IT'S FASTEST TO WRITE OUT EVERYTHING BY HAND FIRST AND THEN TYPE IT INTO THE COMPUTER. I CAN CONTROL THE TAPEDECK WITH MY LEFT HAND WHILE SCRIBBLING FEVERISHLY WITH MY RIGHT.

EDITING

IT'S PERFECTLY IN LINE WITH JOURNALISTIC ETHICS TO CUT OUT BORING PARTS AND REARRANGE THE ORDER OF THE QUESTIONS. THE IMPORTANT THING IS NOT TO DISTORT WHAT THEY SAID. WHENEVER POSSIBLE I LET THE INTERVIEWEE LOOK OVER THE ARTICLE BEFORE PUBLICATION, IF ANYONE IS GOING TO BE ANGRY ABOUT MISQUOTING IT WILL BE THEM.

WHAT TO WEAR

DEFINITELY VELCRO SNAKESKIN BOOTS.

Q&A&YOU

I ALWAYS SPEND A LOT OF TIME WRITING QUESTIONS AND REARRANGING THEM SO THEY FLOW NICELY EVEN THOUGH I NEVER END UP ASKING THEM IN ORDER AND IF EVERYTHING IS GOING WELL I HARDLY LOOK AT MY NOTES AT ALL. THE LESS I LOOK AT THEM THE MORE I'M ABLE TO JUST LISTEN AND RESPOND. STILL IT'S IMPORTANT

CONVERSATION

RESUSCITATE THE LOST ART

HAVE FUN! GOOD LUCK!

BEN BUSH

WHAT BUGS?

Rant and Rave!

Some things just bug. Drive you up the wall! Don't hold it in, get those annoying things down on paper and out the door.

WRITE a **FIRST PERSON** ARGUMENT OR COMPLAINT.

WRITE YOUR **INSPIRATIONS** OR **PERSONAL POINTS** OF **VIEW.**

LET YOUR WORDS BE **COLORED WITH EMOTION.**

SURE, IT'S OPEN TO DISPUTE... Start CONVERSATIONS.

THERE ARE **NO RULES** to YOUR WAY OF LOOKING at THINGS.

SHOO- FLY!

WRITE SIMPLY WHAT SEEMS **TRUE TO YOU.**

no need TO APPOLOGIZE

YOU BUG ME. THAT'S MY JOB. I'M A LITTLE BUGGER.

MY BROTHER, WOODY, ANNOYS ME,

LET'S REVIEW.

EVERYBODY LOVES A CRITIC. OKAY, NOT REALLY.

BUT DON'T LET THAT STOP YOU FROM VOICING YOUR OPINIO
WHY NOT START YOUR OWN REVIEW ZINE? HELP YOUR FAVOR!
ZINESTERS OUT BY LISTING THE BEST ZINES YOU'VE COME ACROSS
(or music, movies, etc.)

HERE'S A GOOD WAY TO GO ABOUT IT...

1. Name of publication to review
   (issue number if any).

2. Name of creator/publisher.

3. The price.

4. The contact mailing address
   and e-mail.

☆ MOST IMPORTANT! TELL READERS HOW THEY
CAN GET A HOLD OF THE ZINES YOU MENTION!

5. Date published.

6. Number of pages.

7. Describe format, size,
   how it was reproduced.

8. Write a brief, to-the-point description.
   Point out your favorite part, highlight any
   suggestions, tell us what you think.
   Be honest and encouraging. Show the world
   the zine you are reviewing has a real
   live beating heart and active brain behind it.

{ Did } BLOGS KILL the Zine Star?

There is something far more personal and intimate about receiving a package in the mail. The widespread access of the web certainly [f]its into the D.I.Y. aesthetic. However, I always feel that too much of anything equals death.
— DAVE KIERSH

THE INTERNET MADE THE DISTRIBUTION, VIEWING AND SHARING OF THE 1000 JOURNALS PROJECT POSSIBLE BUT WITHOUT THE PHYSICAL, TANGIBLE JOURNALS, IT WOULD BE NOTHING MORE THAN A FORUM OF ONLINE COMMENTS.

— BRIAN SINGER (1000 JOURNALS PROJECT)

Blogs can be a refreshing change from the standard layout of a book or a magazine. The messiness factor or "off" quality in a zine can be the most interesting part. I would get rid off all my printed books before my photocopied ones.
— Marc Bell

SAELEE

YOU START TO APPRECIATE A WELL CRAFTED ZINE MORE WHEN YOU KNOW SOMEONE DOESN'T HAVE TO GO TO ALL THE TROUBLE AND CAN JUST START A BLOG.

— SAMMY HARKHAM (KRAMERS ERGOT)

IF ANYTHING, THERE SEEM TO BE MORE ZINES NOW, & IT'S EASIER TO FIND THEM AND TRADE THEM BECAUSE OF THE INTERNET.

(BLOGS SCHMOGS.)

— JORDAN CRANE

MANY PEOPLE WHO HAVE DONE ZINES IN THE PAST ARE DOING BLOGS NOW. I [S]TILL THINK THAT BLOGS AS [A] WHOLE WILL MAKE [PA]PER ZINES BETTER. [T]HE INTERNET IS A GREAT [PL]ACE TO PUBLISH IDEAS & [TH]OUGHTS, & A BLOG CAN BE [US]ED LIKE A PUBLIC DIARY [O]R SKETCH BOOK. — MARK [FI]SCHLER

It probably occurs to the person who decides to make an online thing that it will be cheaper (no printing, no paper, stapling, mailing), and that it could potentially reach more people. Others like the print medium so much so they bite that bullet.
— MARC BELL

I still think that the printed word is just that, meant to be printed.
While blogs may reveal the next great writers and artists, I see print to be very much alive and kicking.

— LOGAN FROM QUIMBY'S BOOKSTORE

REAL ACTUAL PAPER IS NICER TO READ, AND NICER TO HAVE ON YOUR DESK OR BED OR THE BACK OF THE TOILET.

— JORDAN CRANE

PAPER RAD (PAPERRAD.ORG) HAS THE BEST WEBSITE ON THE WEB AND HAS ALSO MADE SOME OF THE BEST ZINES AND COMICS.

— SAMMY HARKHAM (KRAMERS ERGOT)

[AR]T BY: (TOP TO BOTTOM) SOUTHER SALAZAR, SAELEE OH, JORDAN CRANE, MARC BELL, RON REGE, JR., SAMMY HARKHAM

CO-OP!

cooperative,

So if you aren't ready to D.I.A.Y. (Do It All Yourself) then maybe it's time for a cooperative, or co-op. With the help of friends you can contribute as much or as little as your attention span requires. Make it easy and dole out the responsibilities of labor, cost, and ideas equally amongst your posse.

IF YOU ARE...

THEN YOU MAY WANT TO TRY THE ROLE OF...

The Bossy One.

EDITOR

This one is the brains behind the whole project. They have final say and are responsible for finding mistakes and making sure everyone stays true to the subject of the zine.

The Responsible One.

PRODUCTION MANAGER

This person's in charge of getting everyone together and making sure to keep costs down and that everyone turns in their work.

The Artistic One.

ART DIRECTOR

This person's responsible for getting the art and coming up with the look of the cover and inside pages. Has access to art supplies and/or computer with printer.

The Bookworm.

WRITER

This one is responsible for getting the group's ideas down as text. They have a computer, typewriter, or really clear handwriting.

The Clown.

GUY WITH STAPLER

Hey, we all need a laugh, especially when no one can agree on the proper use of "ingenious" vs. "ingenuous." When the laugh's over, hand 'em the stapler.

COOPERATION

Some advice about
working with others:

(from Bwana, the pirate robot.) *

*please note:
the real Bwana is neither
a pirate nor a talking robot.

COPY MACHINE QUARTERS

'MY PERSONAL FEELINGS ARE to iNCluDE PEoPle
iN a way that THEY will Still HaVE an out.
INcludE FRIENDS aND PEERS AS PROOF READERS OR FOR
EDITING OR FaNtastic CONTRiButioNS. BUT
REMEMBER THE MiGHTY, GOLDEN-ENCRUSTED BONUS
TiP: YEE MastERFul CaPtaiN SHould always REMAiN
ONly ONE. ONly ONE FOR THE SMOothEst RiDE." BWaNa SPOONS

Rise and Shine with Saelee Oh and Souther Salazar

Saelee Oh says:

If you're working with a friend on a zine, it's easy to get sidetracked and distracted, so set a time limit for yourselves. It will help you both to concentrate.

Don't feel like anything you contributed is too precious, and be open to things getting cut out or covered over. You can't have a big ego or be too timid in making suggestions, either. A collaboration is more interesting if there are surprises in it for both people.

Working on a zine together is a good way to get to know that guy/girl you have a crush on.

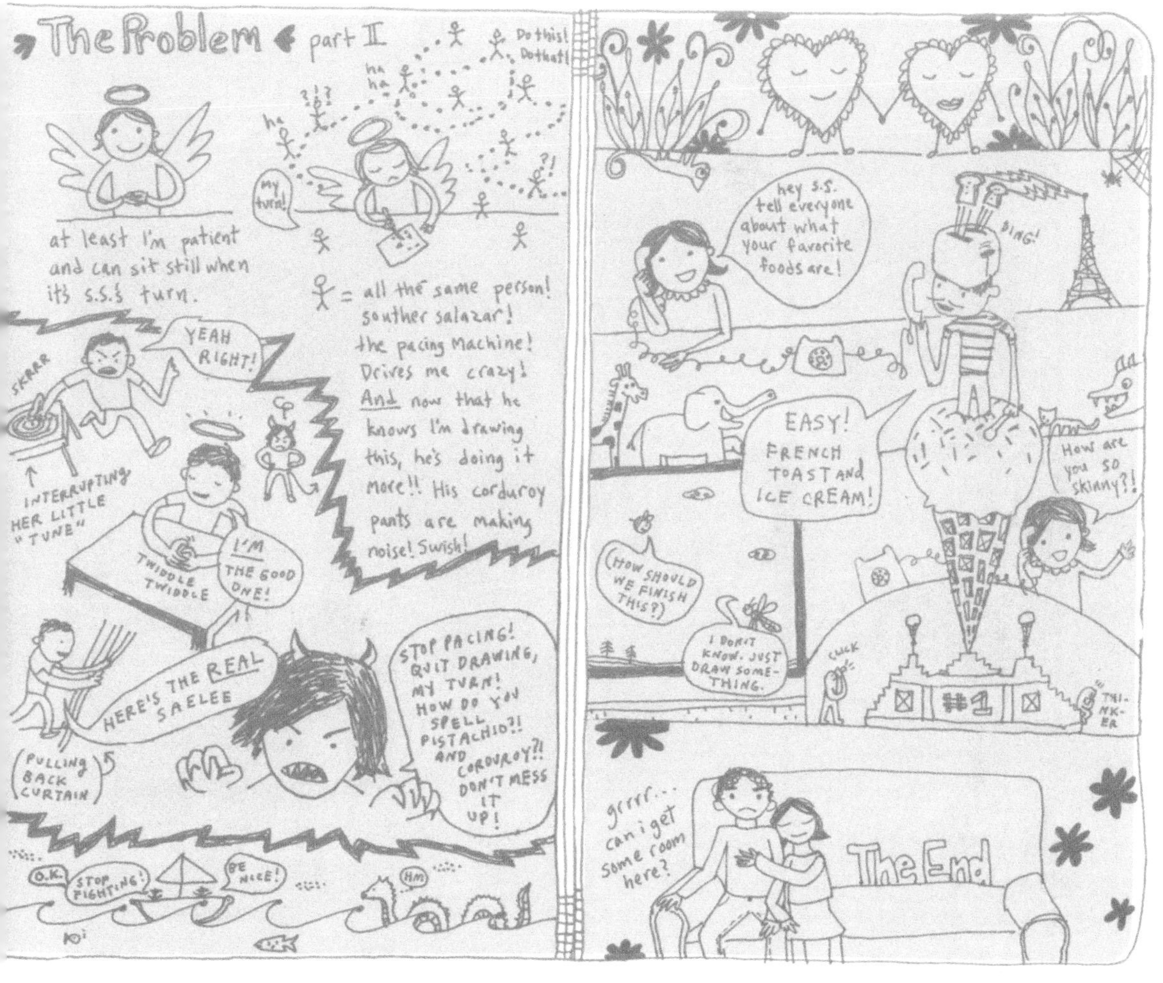
The Problem part II
at least I'm patient and can sit still when it's s.s.'s turn.
my turn!
Do this! Do that!
= all the same person! souther salazar! the pacing machine! Drives me crazy! And now that he knows I'm drawing this, he's doing it more!! His corduroy pants are making noise! Swish!
YEAH RIGHT!
SKRRR
INTERRUPTING HER LITTLE "TUNE"
TWIDDLE TWIDDLE
I'M THE GOOD ONE!
HERE'S THE REAL SAELEE
(PULLING BACK CURTAIN)
STOP PACING! QUIT DRAWING, MY TURN! HOW DO YOU SPELL PISTACHIO?! AND CORDUROY?! DON'T MESS IT UP!
O.K.
STOP FIGHTING!
BE NICE!
HM
hey s.s. tell everyone about what your favorite foods are!
BING!
EASY! FRENCH TOAST AND ICE CREAM!
How are you so skinny?!
(HOW SHOULD WE FINISH THIS?)
I DON'T KNOW. JUST DRAW SOMETHING.
#1
THINKER
grrrr... can i get some room here?
The End

Souther Salazar says:

Sometimes the hardest part when starting a zine with a friend is just getting it started, but you gotta jump right in. Right away, make a mark, any kind of mark on the blank paper in front of you so at least it's not blank anymore. Then pass it on...

Make it like a game. Make up challenges and rewards for finishing sections. Have fun, let each page be what it will be and let it end up in the zine. The imperfections tell the real story.

Try making an entire zine with a PenPal through the mail! It might take 3 or more mailings...

Have a big stack of paper and fill it all up. Try all kinds of different things, something new each time. Trade paper back and forth. Sometimes leave things half finished. What will happen? That's the fun, no one knows. When you are all through, go back and select the best pages and make a zine! The magic is in the strange mix of ideas from more than one brain.

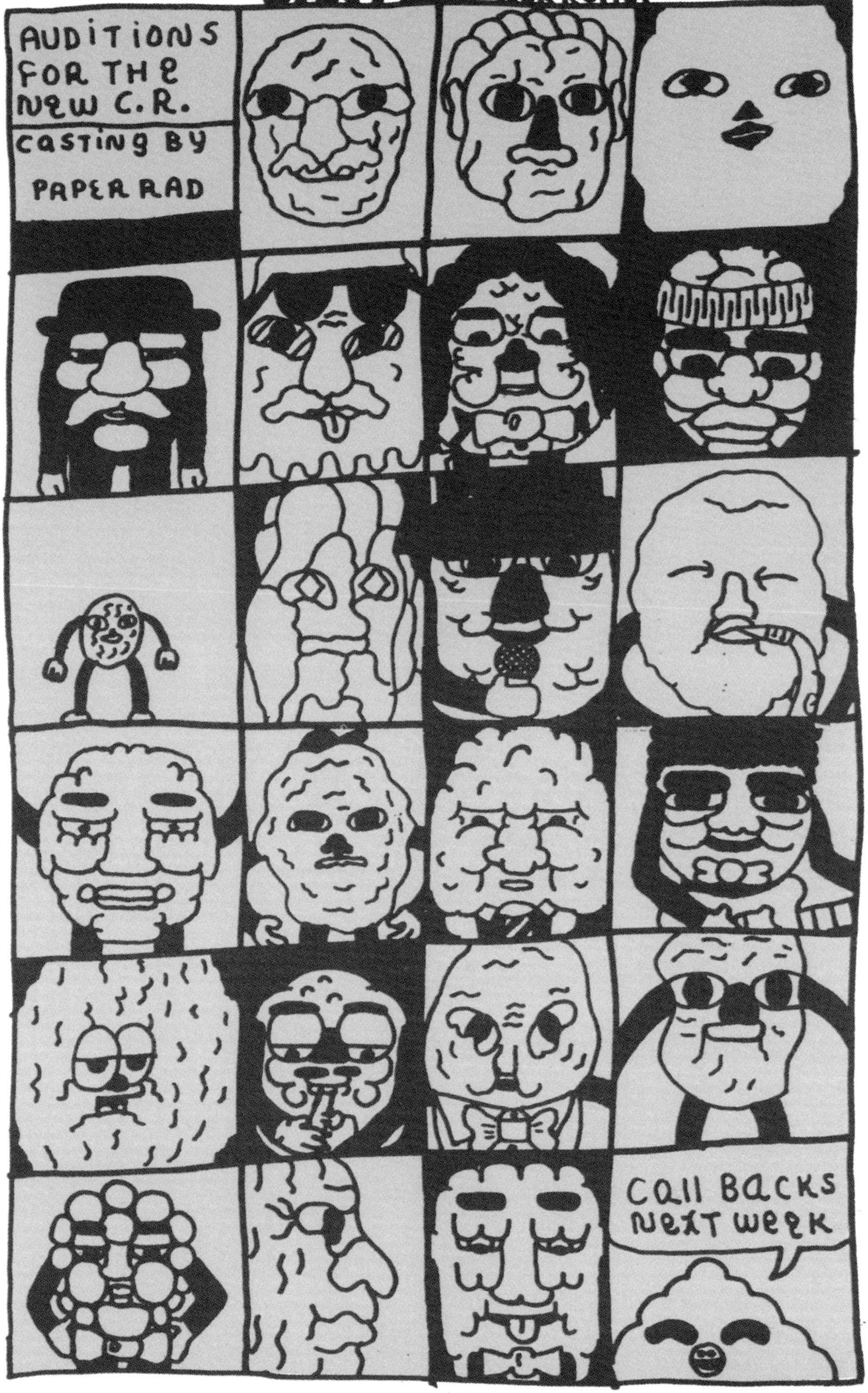
AUDITIONS FOR THE NEW C.R.
CASTING BY PAPER RAD
CALL BACKS NEXT WEEK

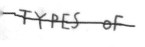 TYPES of

 ZINE

FORMATS:

On the following pages are some patterns and recipes for different zine formats. Each has its own advantages. There are simple ways to make a zine besides the ol' fold-a-piece-of-paper-in-half and staple. If you're looking for more of a challenge try combinations.

THE STANDARD ½ PAGE

no tricks
center bound.

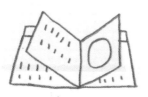

NO STAPLES

¼ PAGE MINI

THE ACCORDIAN

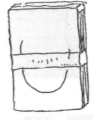

STACK-N-WRAP

for that rubberband
collection.

THE FREEBIE

Why not give something
extra? Stickers, tattoos,
pull-out poster of

Princess Kitty.

THE MICRO-MINI

Zine made from 1
sheet of paper.
The trees thank you.

(a.k.a. El' Cheapo.)

FOLD-N-BIND
French

} Standard ½ page zine. {

Step 1:

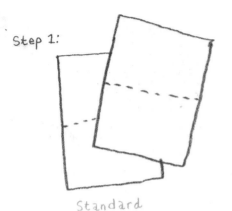

Standard
8½ x 11 paper.

step 2:

Fold

step 3:

INSIDE
COVER

2
3
1

Number the pages.

Step 4:

my
comic

Write and draw.

my
comic

4

✦ Master copies ready to photocopy.

{ This is one of the easiest and
probably the most common
way to make a zine. }

No Staples

step 1: Take 1 11"x17" sheet of paper.

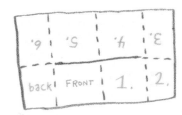

With a pencil, divide into 8 equal parts. number pages in this order.

step 2:

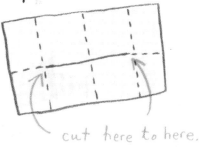

cut here to here.

Step 3: Fold paper lengthways, then the ends like this...

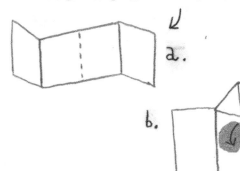

a.

b.

"Pop" center out and away... from each other.

c. the result.

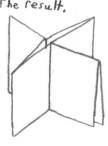

step 4:

Do the art and writing.

step 5:

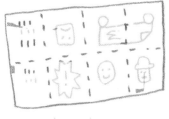

unfold and use as your master copy.

The no-staple formula is a great one, It looks cool, and the way it's constructed makes it super easy — it only needs to be copied on 1 side!

¼ PAGE Mini

Step 1:

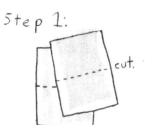

cut.

• cut 2 sheets of paper in half.

Step 2:

stack together.

Step 3:

Fold and staple.

Step 4:

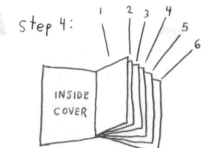

1 2 3 4 5 6

INSIDE COVER

Number the pages.

Step 5:

MY ZINE

Do all the art and writing.

Step 6:

MY ZINE

remove staples.

Step 7:

MY ZINE

Tape sheets back together.
Now it's ready for the copy machine.

This method works great when you want to produce a zine quick and easy, giving you the advantage of working in sequential order.

Micro Mini

Step 1:

Cut 1 sheet of 8½"×11"
paper following A & B.

Step 2:

intro

(YOU SHOULD HAVE 8 SHEETS.)

Stack and fold,

Step 3:

INSIDE COVER

Number pages.

Step 4:

Do all the
art and writing.

Step 5:

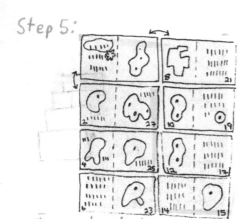

Tape back to
make your master copy.

You can get
a 28 page zine
out of 1 sheet
of paper using
this method.
Wow.
And by following
all the steps
you can work in
sequential order.

One-Step Mini

You can make a copy-ready zine directly on 1 sheet of paper. That way you don't have to mess with all the other steps.

✧ Just make sure you work in this scrambled sequence.

FRONT

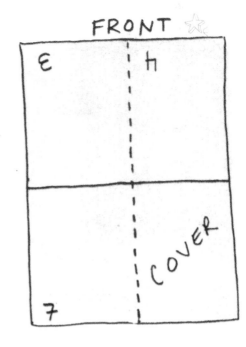

BACK

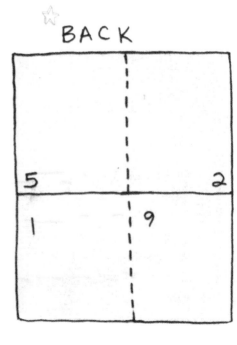

One- Step Micro Mini

This works the same as the one-step standard but you get more pages.

You can work directly on the master copy.

Then cut, fold, and bind after you have made your copies.

Front

COVER	BACK COVER		
		8	21
2	27	10	19
4	25	12	17
6	23	14	15

Step 1:   With a pencil, divide the page.

Step 2:   Do all the art and writing in this scrambled order.

Back

22	7	INSIDE BACK	COVER
20	9	28	1
18	11	26	3
16	13	24	5

~~Draw~~ ~~and~~

~~write~~

The Accordion

(according to us.)

Step 1:

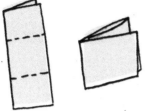

Fold 1 sheet of paper lengthways.

Then into thirds.

Step 2:

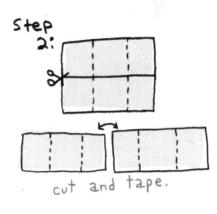

cut and tape.

Step 3:

With a pencil, number your pages like this...

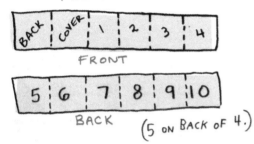

| BACK | COVER | 1 | 2 | 3 | 4 |

FRONT

| 5 | 6 | 7 | 8 | 9 | 10 |

BACK   (5 on BACK of 4.)

Step 4:

Do all the art and writing.

Step 5:

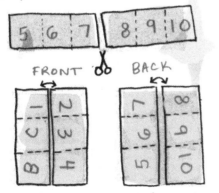

cut and tape back together to make your master copy.

This format is good for paneled comics and free standing display. It doesn't need binding or even an envelope if you want to mail it. Simply fold it up, address it, seal it with a sticker or piece of tape and send it on its way.

You can make all kinds of variations of this format and even use it as an insert for another zine.

The Stack 'n' Wrap

 It's Whack!

step 1:

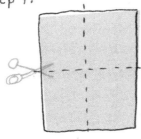

TAKE STANDARD 8½"×11" PAPER AND CUT INTO 4.

Step 2:

Do all the art and writing.

Step 3:

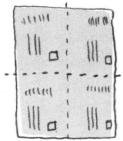

TAPE BACK TOGETHER AND COPY ONTO HEAVY CARD STOCK.

Step 4:

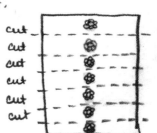

cut cut cut cut cut cut

Be creative and make some wraparound bands with cut paper. (or just use a rubber band.)

Step 5:

GLUE STICK

Bind together

People can recycle your zine as post cards or stickers. So your words and art gets mailed or stuck in all kinds of places!

⟨ The FREEBEE ⟩

❀ Whether it's a fold-out mini-poster, bag of stickers or even an original piece of art, freebees are nice little surprise that add something extra.

☆ Here are some examples...

GIFT BAG

Wheath

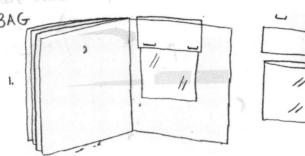

1.

Staple in gift bag. You could use a small sandwich bag or an envelope.

POSTER COVER

DRAW

DUST JACKET

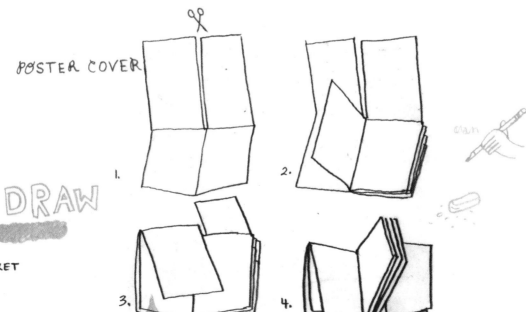

1.

2.

3.

4.

Take a cool drawing or nice patterned print and follow these steps to make a dust jacket that doubles as a poster.

Fold and staple a full page fold-out
into the center of your zine like this...

PULL-OUT POSTER

FREE POSTER

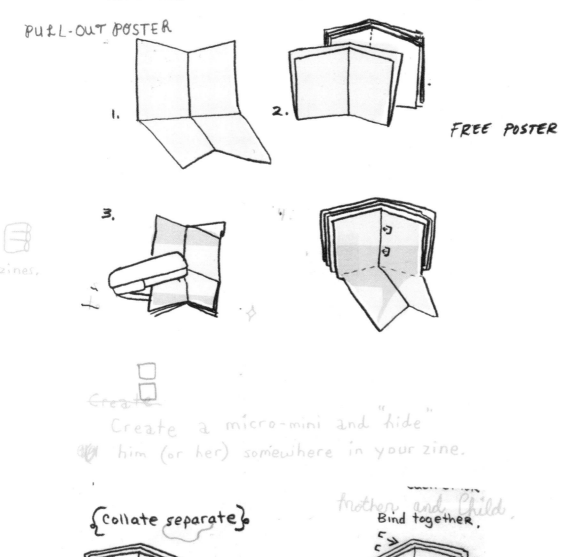

1.

2.

3.

4.

zines.

Create a micro-mini and "hide"
him (or her) somewhere in your zine.

{collate separate}

Mother and child.
Bind together.

BONUS MINI

repeat

make two ZINES
two different sizes.

French Fold 'N' Bind

(a.k.a. The French Connection)

NOT FUNNY.

Step 1:

TAKE STANDARD 8½"x11" PAPER AND CUT IN 2.

cut

Fold... AND STACK TOGETHER.

Step 2:

Binding will go here.

*

Step 3:

Do all the art and writing.

Step 4:

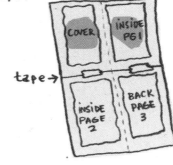

tape →

COVER | INSIDE PG 1
INSIDE PAGE 2 | BACK PAGE 3

Back is blank. One-sided copy keeps costs down!

TAPE BACK TOGETHER TO MAKE YOUR MASTER COPY.

Step 5:

MY COOL ZINE

You can wrap a cover around the french folds if you like.

This is an easy way to make your zine stand out. You can also wrap this zine with a cool cover.

French

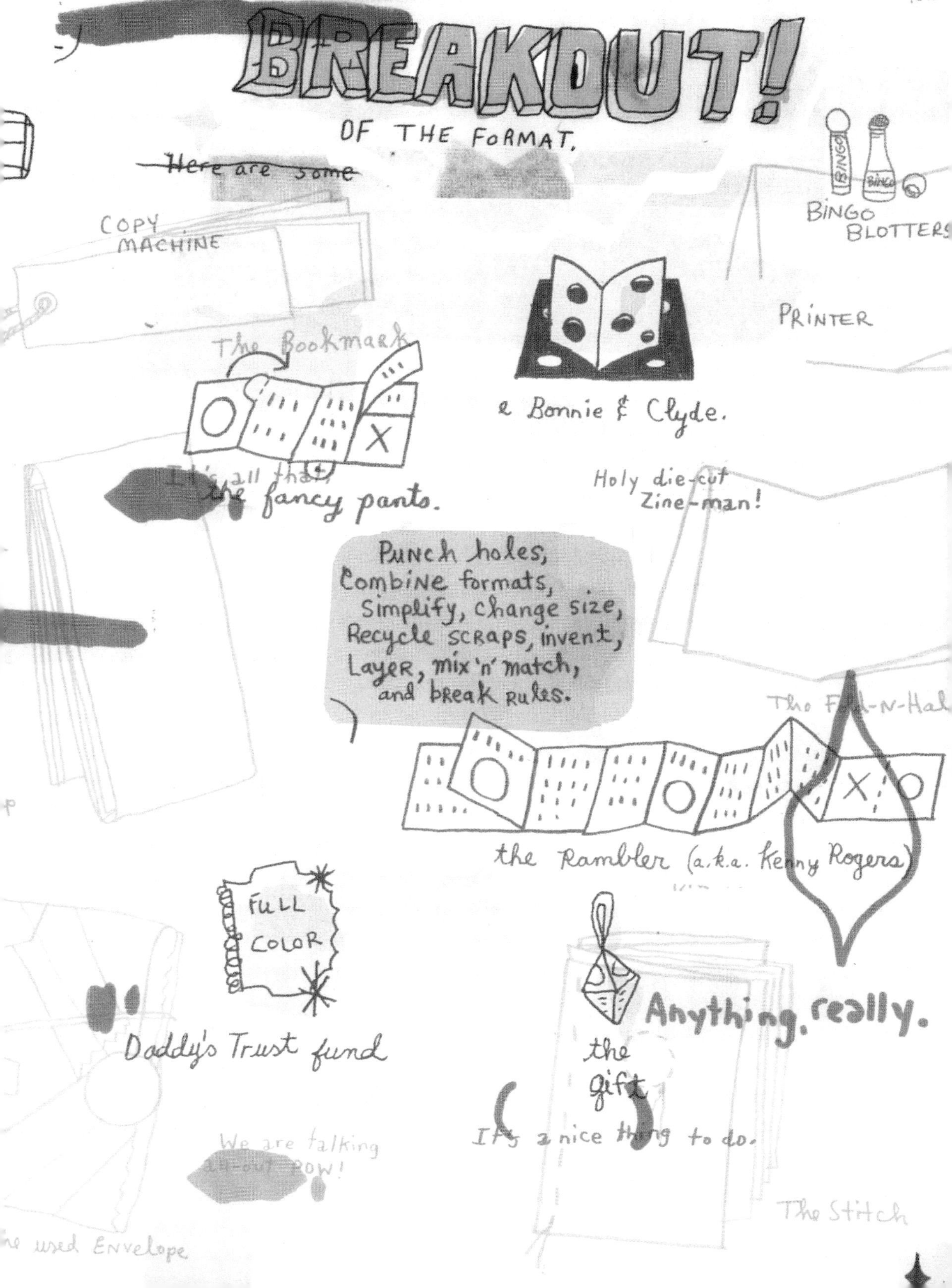
BREAKOUT!
OF THE FORMAT.
~~Here are some~~
COPY MACHINE
BINGO BINGO
BINGO BLOTTERS
PRINTER
The Bookmark
a Bonnie & Clyde.
It's all that
the fancy pants.
Holy die-cut Zine-man!
Punch holes, Combine formats, Simplify, change size, Recycle scraps, invent, Layer, mix 'n' match, and break rules.
the Rambler (a.k.a. Kenny Rogers)
FULL COLOR
Daddy's Trust fund
Anything, really.
the gift
It's a nice thing to do.
We are talking all-out POW!
The Stitch
used Envelope

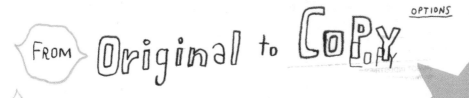

From Original to COPY
OPTIONS

Here are some ways to create copy-ready masters. The darker and more crisp your master is, the better copy you will get.

PENCIL ◇ IF YOU WANT TO STICK TO PENCIL, USE A SOFTER LEAD LIKE A 4B RATHER THAN A STANDARD NO.2

(AVAIL. AT ART STORES FOR ABOUT $1)

Some people use a non-photo blue pencil. By using it, your sketch lines will not appear when photocopied. (available at art stores for about $1.29)

BALL-POINT ◇ CAN PHOTOCOPY STREAKY.

(PENCIL OR BALL-POINT WILL PROBABLY NEED TO BE SET TO COPY DARKER.)

MARKERS ◇ USE A COMBINATION OF MARKERS, THIN AND THICK, TO SAVE TIME AND GET BETTER RESULTS.

INK AND BRUSH ◇ PERFECT FOR FILLING IN LOTS OF BLACK AREAS. USE A SMALL BRUSH (SIZE 0 or SMALLER) FOR FINE LINES AND BETTER CONTROL.

(A BOTTLE OF WATERPROOF INK AND A FEW BRUSHES WILL COST YOU AROUND $10.)

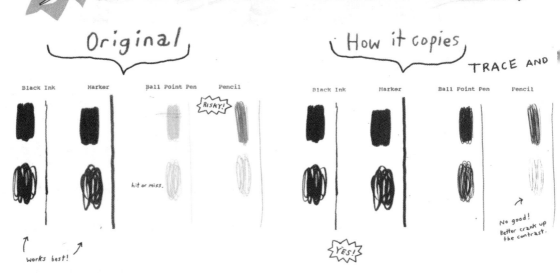

Original — How it copies

TRACE AND

| Black Ink | Marker | Ball Point Pen | Pencil | Black Ink | Marker | Ball Point Pen | Pencil |

RISKY!

hit or miss.

works best!

YES!

No good! Better crank up the contrast.

to get a good print, try
one of these options.

OPTION 1:

1. SKETCH IN PENCIL.

2. INK IT IN.

OPTION 2:

USE A LIGHTBOX.

STEP 1.

CREATE A LOOSE
SKETCH IN PENCIL.

2. TIGHTEN UP
THE SKETCH ON
A LIGHTBOX.

3. THEN INK IT IN.

ADD CONTRAST.

OPTION 3: COMPUTER

STEP 1: DRAW IN PENCIL, (# 4B is best.)

2: SCAN INTO COMPUTER.

3. ADJUST, CORRECT AND DARKEN,

4: PRINT OUT

END RESULT.

MASTER COPY

Once you have your art and writing set in a zine format your master copy is ready for testing. Make sure to check for spelling (if you want), and darken light spots.

DARKEN A BIT.

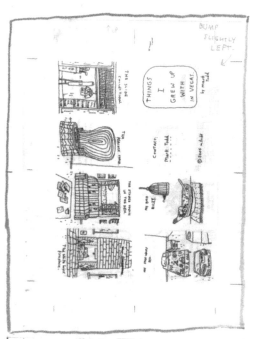

BUMP SLIGHTLY LEFT.

FRONT

CUT

BACK

Save yourself some time and money by first running a test copy, checking how it ~~all line~~ lines up and that the pages are in order. Some small ~~pieces~~ happy accidents can turn out to be cool.

SPELLING?

SHIFT →

CENTER AT 5.5"

Cropping

NEED TO LOWER COVER ART.

SAMPLE COPY CUT AND STAPLED.

CHECK FOR CROPPING.

Double UP

◆ with a little bit of planning ahead, you can get more bang for your buck.

A.

8½ × 11 Sheet of paper.

↓

Result: For every copy you get 2 zines.

B.

8½ × 11 Sheet of paper.

↓

Result: For every copy you get 3 zines.

COPIER TRICKS

because... it's fun.

The copy machine can be a great tool for making art. You can enlarge, reduce, and blur to come up with images you wouldn't have without experimentation. Below are some simple copy machine screw-arounds you can start with and build upon. We laid out the process with our end results so you can see just how much you can do with the copier tool keys. All copy machines are different and they all have their own advantages and disadvantages. What we have learned is the more steps you take and invent to get that one perfect image, the better the outcome.

Remember: most copy machines leave a border and will crop off the edge of your image. Our way around the border is to make sure there is white around the edge, push the border erase button if the machine has one or reduce the master copy then trim after collating.

NORMAL Copy.

high contrast copy of crumpled art

drag while copying

drag while copying using color toner

⑲ .. the CLIFFS

Troy knew of a secret place on the way to Lake Mead. It was hard to find, you had to drive down lots of winding dirt roads. If the road signs were shot out it meant that you were going the right way. The cliffs were just that - big cliffs that you could climb and jump off of into the lake. Troy liked to hang out at the cliffs, it was a place to meet people, impress girls and smoke freely.

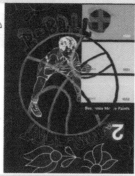

INVERT,

⑲ .. the CLIFFS

Troy knew of a secret place on the way to Lake Mead. It was hard to find, you had to drive down lots of winding dirt roads. If the road signs were shot out it meant that you were going the right way. The cliffs were just that - big cliffs that you could climb and jump off of into the lake. Troy liked to hang out at the cliffs, it was a place to meet people, impress girls and smoke freely.

enlarged 200% + 200%

copy of a copy.

⑲ .. the CLIFFS

Troy knew of a secret place on the way to Lake Mead. It was hard to find, you had to drive down lots of winding dirt roads. If the road signs were shot out it meant that you were going the right way. The cliffs were just that - big cliffs that you could climb and jump off of into the lake. Troy liked to hang out at the cliffs, it was a place to meet people, impress girls and smoke freely.

enlarged 200% + 200% + 200%

⑲ .. the CLIFFS

Troy knew of a secret place on the way to Lake Mead. It was hard to find, you had to drive down lots of winding dirt roads. If the road signs were shot out it meant that you were going the right way. The cliffs were just that - big cliffs that you could climb and jump off of into the lake. Troy liked to hang out at the cliffs, it was a place to meet people, impress girls and smoke freely.

enlarged

200% + 200% + 200% + 200%

⑲ .. the CLIFFS

Troy knew of a secret place on the way to Lake Mead. It was hard to find, you had to drive down lots of winding dirt roads. If the road signs were shot out it meant that you were going the right way. The cliffs were just that - big cliffs that you could climb and jump off of into the lake. Troy liked to hang out at the cliffs, it was a place to meet people, impress girls and smoke freely.

200% + 200% + 200% + 200% + 200%

enlarged

y of a copied copy

⑲ .. the CLIFFS

Troy knew of a secret place on the way to Lake Mead. It was hard to find, you had to drive down lots of winding dirt roads. If the road signs were shot out it meant that you were going the right way. The cliffs were just that - big cliffs that you could climb and jump off of into the lake. Troy liked to hang out at the cliffs, it was a place to meet people, impress girls and smoke freely.

+ 200% 200% + 200%

enlarged 200% + 200% + 200%

COPY TALK ★ PLUS!
(WEIRD NIGHT AT THE COPY STORE)
BY KARYN RAZ!

PAPER SIZES FOR THE PHOTOCOPY MACHINE.

8½x11" Standard
8½x14 Legal
11x17 Tabloid
12x18

weary italian
couple argue about
a xeroxing project.

Si!! No!
Si. Na
Si?
No?
Si.?

We asked the local copy guy about paper weights.

US: "WHAT'S THE THICKEST PAPER A COPIER WILL RUN?"

HIM: "IT'S NOT JUST THE (WEIGHT) OR THICKNESS OF THE PAPER THAT'S A FACTOR, ITS ALSO THE TYPE OF PAPER. A HEAVYWEIGHT CARDSTOCK MAY RUN BETTER THAN A LIGHTER GLOSSY PAPER."   US: "THANKS."

The thickness of paper in the U.S. is determined by its weight.
The higher the number, the thicker (or heavier) the paper.

⭢ REG. COPY PAPER IS ABOUT 20 lbs. while cardstock is around 110 lbs.

IF YOU PLAN ON USING ANY TYPE OF PAPER OTHER THAN REG. COPY PAPER,

TIP:- IT'S ALMOST ALWAYS BEST TO BRING YOUR OWN. SAVES MONEY.

{EXPERIMENT!} TRY ALL TYPES OF PAPERS.

NEWSPRINT, HEAVY CARDSTOCK, TRACING PAPER, GRID PAPER,...

∅ NEVER PUT INKJET PAPER OR PLASTIC INTO A COPY MACHINE.

TIP: ⭢ BRING EXTRA PAPER. IF YOU NEED 100 COPIES, THEN BRING 125 SHEETS. ALWAYS FACTOR IN JAM-UPS, MESS-UPS AND OTHER TYPES OF UPS.)

U.S.A.

TIP: ⭢ IF YOU BRING YOUR OWN PAPER, BRING THE PACKAGING IT CAME IN. COPY STORES USUALLY WANT TO KNOW EXACTLY WHAT THEY'RE RUNNING IN THEIR VERY EXPENSIVE MACHINES.

BLACK-AND-WHITE:

B/W COPIERS WERE DESIGNED TO COPY TEXT, PURE BLACK AND WHITE. SO IF YOUR ZINE HAS TONES OF GRAY, YOU MAY NEED TO TRY ADJUSTING THE COPIER SETTINGS UNTIL YOU GET A DECENT RESULT.

SOME B/W COPIERS HAVE COLOR OPTIONS. IF YOU CAN FIND ONE OF THOSE, YOU'VE STRUCK **GOLD** BECAUSE YOU CAN GET COLOR COPIES FOR THE COST OF A BLACK-AND-WHITE COPY!

Lady in trench coat laughs manically while making strange scrawls.

COLOR:

A LOT OF PLACES HAVE SELF-SERVICE COLOR COPIERS THESE DAYS. YOU CAN HAVE A LOT OF FUN WITH COLOR, ESPECIALLY IF THE COPIER DOESN'T HAVE A COUNTER ON IT. BECAUSE THEY CAN GET EXPENSIVE.

(IF IT HAS A COPY COUNTER, YOU'RE GOING TO BE CHARGED FOR ALL THOSE "TEST" COPIES.)

They sure weigh down these tape dispensers, Ruby.

Ancient Couple prepares to send out their bills.

oversize COPIERS:

→ Oversize copy machines are cool. You can make HUGE copies for pretty cheap.

36 inches wide and just about as long as you want. about 70¢ a square foot.
(because it prints on a continuous roll)

They even make oversize COLOR copiers.
They're pricey but imagine how a GIANT color copy would look!
(about $10 a sq. ft. and they can go 60" wide!)

◇ — You could make the world's largest zine!

◇ — You could cut the giant copy into tons of mini baby zines.

◇ — You could fold it up and make a zine Map!

☆ — DESIGNING YOUR ZINE ON THE COMPUTER, USING A LAYOUT PROGRAM, AND GIVING A DISK WITH PDF FILES TO THE COPY STORE FOR OUTPUT IS GOING TO GIVE YOU THE BEST QUALITY COPIES.

(YES, LINES WILL BE CRISP, TONES SUBTLE. BUT SOMETIMES YOU JUST WANT TO GO IN, MAKE SOME FUN ZINES, DOWN AND DIRTY, FAULTS AND ALL, AND BE DONE WITH IT.)

Matt comes & rescues me. He's dressed in a dapper work outfit, while I'm in schlumpy art-school bum mode. And it's only week 3.

Employee discusses how he spent the night before puking & making his girlfriend clean it up.

THE POOR MAN'S PRINTER

If you can find a black-and-white copier with color toner you can come up with a cheap alternative to offset printing. Some copy machines have separate toner that comes in blue, green, and/or red and brown. Some copiers only have ~~ENER~~ one color, some have more than one. With a little luck and a lot of patience you can get some really cool results by experimenting. Don't try too hard to get the color to line up just right. It's nearly impossible and if it is off a bit it will look much better in the end. Most copiers have a bypass tray so that you can keep feeding the same sheet of paper through again and again.

ORIGINAL

by MARK Todd & Esther Pearl Watson

make a high-contrast copy and feed copy back into bypass tray.

select color toner and copy image b over copy a.

end result.

by MARK Todd & Esther Pearl Watson

by MARK Todd & Esther Pearl Watson

make a high-contrast copy and feed copy back into bypass tray.

select color toner and copy image b over copy a.

end result

 +  +  =

make a high-contrast
copy and feed copy back

into bypass tray,

select color
toner and
copy image b over
copy a and feed back
into bypass tray.

cut out type, set
toner to b/w,

copy over

image a and b.

end result.

result

 +  +  =

make a high-contrast
copy and feed copy back

into bypass tray.

select color
toner and
copy image b over
copy a and feed back
into bypass tray.

select black toner
and copy over image
a and b.

end result.

Make several copies of your original art, then cut out different parts
and re-copy them all back together by feeding them through the bypass tray.
Do a lot of tests, change the order you make the copies, adjust the
contrast. The last image you copy usually stands out the most since it's
sitting on top of the rest.   And you don't have to stick to using white
copier paper, either. Try colored papers, lined school notebook paper, etc.
You can't go too thick or glossy or the machine may jam up. You don't
need to necessarily copy your entire zine this way — it usually
works best for covers or on sections of the book.

THE DITTO MACHINE. BY

TAKE ONE...PASS IT ON AND ON AND ON AND ON

BEFORE THE XEROX CORPORATION FLEXED ITS MIGHTY TONER MUSCLES,
SPIRIT DUPLICATORS WERE WIDELY USED THROUGHOUT THE EDUCATIONAL
INDUSTRY FOR ITS TEST, QUIZ, AND DOCUMENT PRINTING NEEDS.
IF THE COPIES WERE FRESH, STUDENTS WOULD PRESS THE "RUN-OFFS"
OR "HAND-OUTS" TO THEIR FACES AND INHALE THE HIGH-INDUCING VAPORS

circle one only!

school   spirit   "HIGH"   76

A.B. DICK IS A COMPANY THAT SELLS THE PURPLE SPIRIT MASTERS
AND THE GALLONS AND GAL LONS OF SPIRIT FLUID FUN THAT
IS CURRENTLY STILL AVAILABLE.

SOME SPIRIT DUPLICATORS CAN BE MANUALLY HAND-CRANKED. QUITE SIMPLY,
YOU NEVER "GO OUT OF POWER." INFORMATION HAS TO COME FROM SOMEWHERE.
WHY NOT FROM YOU? THE TRUTH IS NEVER BLACK-AND-WHITE. IT'S PURPLE.

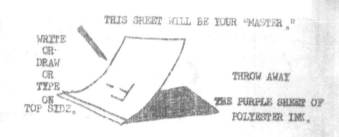

THIS SHEET WILL BE YOUR "MASTER."

WRITE
OR
DRAW
OR
TYPE
ON
TOP SIDE.

THROW AWAY

THE PURPLE SHEET OF
POLYESTER INK.

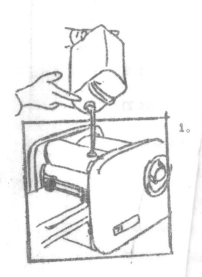

1. START WITH GOOD QUALITY SPIRIT FLUID.

A CARBON "MASTER" CAN BE TYPED OR WRITTEN OR SCRATCHED ON

THE "MASTER" WRAP AROUND THE DRUM IN THE MACHINE.

AS THE DRUM TURNS, THE MASTER IS COATED WITH THE "SPIRIT"

FLUID VIA A WICK THAT IS BEING SOAKED WITH THE FLUID.

AS PAPER IS PASSED THROUGH THE MACHINE, IT PRESSES

AGAINST THE WET MASTER ON THE DRUM AND SOME OF THE PURPLE

INK IS IMPRINTED.

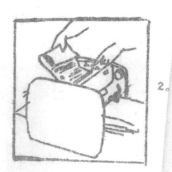

2. SECRET INK? MYTHICAL "HIGH" ?

GHOST PAPER ?

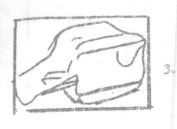

3. COVER MACHINE.

{ IMAGE is EVERYTHING. }

Here is a page from Mark's Magazine, Malcolm.
It shows the process he used to create the final layout.

I like to draw my art by hand
then scan it into the computer.
Once there I can make simple changes
digitally, and piece drawings   together
if I want to. The first drawing I did was
directly onto the ¼ mini but drawing
so   many details so small wasn't
easy. I did not like the end result.

So, I drew a picture in pencil on an
8½x11" sheet of paper. The details
looked much more crisp once the
drawing was reduced down.

Some prefer Bitmap.
With bitmap the image will be
pure black and white, no grays
or tones.

(Bitmap= 100%.
black + white,
no grays.)

Using a computer,

I scanned my art at 300 dpi in grayscale.
In   Photoshop, I adjusted the levels to
make the darks darker and the lights lighter,
but I didn't blow it out completely because
I liked the smudges and smears.

Bitmap   Grayscale

Scan at least 600 dpi   Scan at least 300 dpi
and save as a TIFF.   and save as a TIFF.

for detailed information on
Bitmap and Grayscale for minicomics
check out   the downloadable pdf
"A Guide to REproduction" by Jordan Crane,
Ron R ge Jr., Dave Choe, and Brian Ralph.
http://www.reddingk.com/reproguide.pdf

The final image was going
to be printed professionaly
and I wanted to add some
simple color to the piece.
In Photoshop, I created a
new layer and drew some
solid black shapes in the
computer. I printed the
"color layer" and line art
separately and chose a
PMS color.

(the printer usually has
a good selection of inks
to choose from. It will

cost you a bit more to
request a custom color.)

This is the end result I
got from the printer. A simple
2 color process (brown and
100% black) on a color paper
stock. This combination kept
my costs down

It is an inexpensive and easy
approach that can have strong
graphic appeal.

i don't really know.

GO PRO!

TAKING YOUR ZINE TO A PRINTER.

by Mark Dischler

AFTER YOU'VE PRINTED A FEW ZINES AT THE COPY STORE, YOU'RE A PRO AT CUT AND PASTE, AND YOU'VE SAVED UP ALL YOUR MONEY AND WANT TO HAVE YOUR BOOK PRINTED UP BY A PROFESSIONAL. WHAT'S THE NEXT STEP?

You may be asking, "How do I make sure I'll get the most for my money?"

or "How do I figure out what to get when there are so many option & so much to learn about the printing process?"

→ Well, you don't need to be an expert. Just use this list of printing terms & specs & you'll know enough to get you started:

PAGE COUNT

Generally, printers work in multiples of 16. So your zine can be 16, 32, 48, 64...or even up to 128 pages!

ZINE SIZE

Using a non-standard size can give your zine a unique look, but going bigger than magazine size could get costly. Here's a basic rundown of what you'd see at a newsstand:

BASIC MAGAZINE - 8 1/4" x 10 3/4"
COMIC BOOK - 6 5/8" x 10 1/4"
TV GUIDE - 5" x 7 3/8"

Here are some popular zine formats:

STANDARD 1/2 PAGE ZINE - 5 1/2" x 8 1/2"
MINI 1/4 PAGE ZINE - 4 1/2" x 5 1/2"

PAPER STOCK

All printers offer a variety of papers. The thickness or weight of the paper stock is measured in pounds and is abbreviated as "lbs", or with the "#" si
Examples of common paper stock include:

TRACING PAPER - 17#   COPY PAPER - 20#   NEWSPRINT - 30#

LINEN RESUME PAPER - 70#   INDEX CARD - 110#

ADDING COLOR

Mom-and-pop print shops and commercial printers produce large amounts of printed material quickly using the process known as "offset printing." Producing full color artwork with offset printing is costly, so for your zine you may want to limit it to one or two colors maximum. When using two colors, the first color is for text and the line drawings. A darker color works best. The second color or "spot color" is used to add tone and contrast underneath the first color.

MAKING FLATS

There are two ways to create high-quality "print ready" artwork
for the printer to use. One way is to provide laser printouts of
all the text and line art as well as any original photographs at
exact size of the book. The other way is to scan in all of the
artwork and photos and deliver it to the printer at least 300 dpi on
a disk or CD.   (dots per inch)

A BIT about CUTTING, BLEEDS, MARGINS, AND BINDING

Book pages are printed and folded on large sheets of paper
and then cut and bound. The margin outside ▬ the cutting area
is called bleed. xi If you want your artwork to go all the
way to the edge of the page, you'll need it to be x larger
than the actual size of the finished book. How much larger?
From 1/8" to 1/4" larger.

Margins are also an important part of book design. Depending
on how you bind your zine, either with a single or double
"stitch" (staple) or with a glue binding, you should always
add extra space in the margin on the inside edge of each page.

holy

GETTING A QUOTE (PRICE)

No two printers have the exact same equipment or materials,
so be prepared to ask questions, make compromises, and haggle
the price. Once the specs are decided on , it is customary for
the printer to write up an itemized quote that summarizes every
aspect of the book and printing process. Get quotes from a few
different printers. Shop around and gain valuable knowledge and
experience.

QUANTiTY

The more you print, the cheaper each individual book will
cost. Print runs are commonly done in groups of 500.
To get a better idea of overall cost it's best to get a
quote for two quantities. For a first-timer, get a quote for
500 books and 1000 books.

— THAT SHOULD BE MORE THAN ENOUGH!

PROOFS

Before the plates are burned for the printing press, your
printer will create a set of proofs that show you how your
book will look based on the flats(print-ready pages) you send
them and the specs in the quote. After you get the proofs
you can make last minute changes or adjustments before it goes
to press. (THEY MAY WANT TO CHARGE EXTRA FOR THIS.)

        Once you approve the proof, the printer sets
everything up and does the print run. Now sit back and wait.
You'll get your finished books in a few weeks.

HOW TO MAKE A SILKSCREEN-PRINTED ZINE COVER

with two colors in 10 Hyper-Steps

YOU'LL NEED:

- TWO SCREENS *
- PHOTO-SENSITIVE EMULSION *
- SQUEEGEE *
- PACKAGING TAPE
- INKS (WATER-BASED) *
- LIGHT SOURCE FOR EXPOSURE (SUNLIGHT, UV LAMP, HALOGEN, ETC) *
- SPACE (AN AREA SET ASIDE FOR A DAY OR SO)
- SPRAY BOTTLE (RECYCLED HOUSEHOLD CLEANER BOTTLE)
- PRINT CLAMPS *
- MASKING TAPE
- PAPER TOWELS
- SPATULA

- LONG ARM STAPLER
- EMULSION SCOOP *
- AMBER BULB, DARK ROOM LIGHT (AVAILABLE FROM PHOTO SUPPLY STORES) *
- TIMER (FOR EXPOSURE TIME)
- BLACK HEAVY-WEIGHT TRASH BAG
- WEIGHTS (CINDER BLOCKS, BRICKS, ETC.) OR SHEET OF GLASS
- BLACK PAPER BOARD
- PROPYLENE GLYCOL *
- BLACK ELECTRICAL TAPE (OPTIONAL)
- PLASTIC TUB
- NEWSPAPER
- PAPER (SOME KIND OF PRINTABLE MATERIAL)
- A SHEET OF GLASS FOR LIGHT-ABOVE EXPOSURE METHOD (WITH TAPED PROTECTIVE EDG...)

* ASK YOUR LOCAL KNOWLEDGEABLE PRINT/ART SUPPLY STORE.

2) COAT SCREENS WITH EMULSION

YOU'LL NEED TO PREPARE THE SCREENS WITH EMULSION TO BE EXPOSED TO LIGHT IN ORDER TO BURN AN IMAGE TO PRINT. IN A DARKROOM LIT WITH AN AMBER LIGHT (OR SPECIAL LIGHT THAT DOESN'T EXPOSE THE PHOTO-EMULSION)...

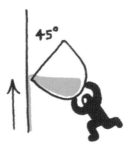

45°

MIX YOUR EMULSION.
POUR SOME MIXED-EMULSION IN A SCOOP

SPREAD EMULSION — PRESS THE TOP EDGE OF THE SCOOP TO THE SCREEN SURFACE,
TILT SCOOP AT ABOUT A 45° DEGREE ANGLE, AND DRAG UPWARDS.

180°

STOP AT THE TOP OF THE SCREEN AND TURN SCOOP
WHILE KEEPING CONTACT WITH THE EDGE OF THE
SCOOP TO THE SCREEN SURFACE SO THE EMULSION
IS LEVEL, THEN PULL SCOOP AWAY. THE EMULSION
SHOULD PULL ONTO THE SCREEN AS A THIN,
SMOOTH SURFACE.

TURN THE SCREEN AROUND 180 DEGREES SO THE THICK
EDGE DOESN'T DRIP INTO YOUR SCREEN MIDDLE.

POUR REMAINING EMULSION BACK INTO THE
STORAGE CONTAINER. (YOU CAN WRAP THE
EMULSION CONTAINER WITH BLACK ELECTRICAL
TAPE TO PROTECT IT FROM EXPOSURE.)

SCREENS DRY FOR AT LEAST AN HOUR OR SO. STOCKPILE SCREENS FOR FUTURE USE. STORE THEM IN BLACK PLASTIC BAGS IN A COOL, DRY, DARK PLACE (CLOSETS, BASEMENTS, OF GARAGE, UNDER A BED, ETC.)

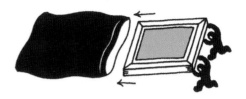

DESIGN YOUR LAYOUT

E WHILE YOUR SCREENS ARE DRYING YOU CAN PUT TOGETHER YOUR ARTWORK. THE POSSIBILITIES FOR COLORS, SIZES, MATERIALS AND MORE ARE ENDLESS. FOR DEMONSTRATION SES, WE'RE GOING TO PUT TOGETHER A TWO-COLOR DESIGN ON AN 8½ × 11 THICK PIECE OF PAPER.

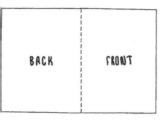

BACK	FRONT

BACK	FRONT

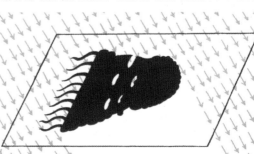

YOUR PAPER AND FOLD IT IN HALF. THIS IS YOUR CANVAS AREA TO EXPERIMENT AND WORK OUT YOUR
. THERE ARE MANY WAYS OF DOING THIS; SUCH AS DRAWING DIRECTLY ON THE PAPER BY HAND, USING
OPIES AS COLLAGE ON THE PAPER, OR USING A COMPUTER LAYOUT WITH THE SAME DIMENSIONS. WHEN
WING, BE SURE TO LEAVE AN INCH OR SO OF SPACE AROUND THE EDGE SO THE IMAGE
TRANSFER COMPLETELY.

COLOR A   +   COLOR B   =

WE'RE GOING TO MAKE A BASIC COVER WITH TITLE, ARTWORK, AND AUTHOR/ARTIST NAME.

COLOR WILL NEED ITS OWN SCREEN, SO WE'LL MAKE A LAYER FOR COLOR A AND COLOR B.

MAKE A FILM POSITIVE

N THE ART IS READY, PHOTOCOPY OR LASER PRINT IT ONTO ACETATE. (GOOD COPY SHOPS WILL DO THIS.) THE BLACK AREAS WILL SHIELD THE PHOTO EMULSION
THE LIGHT, SO MAKE SURE THEY ARE AS BLACK AS POSSIBLE. YOU MAY WANT TO DOUBLE UP THE PHOTOCOPIES TO BE SURE. (IT'S SUGGESTED TO *DOUBLE UP YOUR COPIES*
USE THE THINNER THE LINES THE MORE TRANSPARENT THE DARKS BECOME. THE EXTRA LAYER WILL ELIMINATE UNWANTED LIGHT FILTERING INTO YOUR IMAGE.)

(EXAMPLE: LIGHT
SOURCE FROM ABOVE)

5) EXPOSE THE SCREENS

PUT YOUR FILM POSITIVE ON THE EMULSION-COATED SCREEN. THE BLACK AREAS SHIELD THE EMULSION FROM THE LIGHT SO THAT IT DOESN'T HARDEN WHERE YOU DON'T IT TO. IT'LL TAKE A FEW TRIES UNTIL YOU LEARN HOW MUCH TIME IT TAKES TO EXPOSE YOUR EMULSION.

FOR SUN:

FOR UV EXPOSURE UNIT:

A PIECE OF GLASS ON TOP OF THE FILM (ACETATE)

6) CLEAN SCREEN

AFTER THE LIGHT EXPOSURE, REMOVE THE FILM POSITIVES AND SPRAY YOUR SCREENS WITH WATER FROM A SPRAY BOTTLE, WAIT A FEW MINUTES FOR THE WATER TO SOFTEN THE UNEXPOSED AREAS (THE PARTS COVERED BY THE DARK AREAS OF YOUR DESIGN). SPRAY OUT THE SOFT, UNEXPOSED EMULSION WITH A HOSE.

7) SET UP TO PRINT

WHILE THE SCREENS ARE DRYING, PUT AWAY THE UNEXPOSED SCREENS (IN BLACK PLASTIC BAGS). NOW YOU CAN TURN ON THE REGULAR LIGHTS. MIX THE INK (YOU CAN USE PROPYLENE GLYCOL TO SLOW DOWN THE DRYING, SO THE SCREEN DOESN'T GET PLUGGED UP AS QUICKLY). PLACE YOUR PRINTABLE PAPER IN A REACHABLE AREA. MAKE SURE YOU HAVE A STACK OF NEWSPAPERS AND PAPER TOWELS NEARBY. YOU MAY WANT TO COVER AREAS WITH NEWSPAPER IN CASE OF INK SPILLAGE OR DRIPS. WHEN THE SCREEN IS DRY, TAPE THE EDGE OF THE SCREEN TO SEAL IT (AND PREVENT UNWANTED INK LEAKAGE). PUT THE SCREEN IN THE CLAMPS AND LINE IT UP TO THE PAPER. USE THE MASKING TAPE TO OUTLINE THE PAPER SO YOU KNOW WHERE TO PLACE IT.

8) PRINT AND PRINT AGAIN

FINALLY, YOU GET TO PRINT! DAB THE SCREEN WITH A LITTLE WATER AND PAPER TOWEL. POUR INK ON THE SCREEN AND PULL THE SQUEEGEE.

LIFT AND PROP UP SCREEN (WITH A ROLL OF TAPE OR SMALL OBJECT).   THERE'S THE FIRST PRINTED LAYER OF YOUR COVER.   LATER... YOUR SECOND PRINTED LAYER OF YOUR COVER.

COLOR A   COLOR A + COLOR B

PUT THIS ON A DRYING RACK OR FLAT SURFACE (TABLE, FLOOR, ANYWHERE IT CAN SAFELY DRY). WHILE YOU'RE PRINTING, INK WILL BEGIN TO DRY ON THE SCREEN AND PLUG IT UP. PUT A FEW PAPER TOWELS UNDERNEATH, PUT THE SCREEN DOWN, AND SPRAY THE ART AREA ON THE SCREEN LIGHTLY WITH WATER. LIGHTLY DAB WITH MORE PAPER TOWELS. REMOVE THE PAPER TOWELS AND TEST PRINT ON THE NEWSPAPERS (THIS WAY YOU DON'T WASTE YOUR GOOD PAPER). WHEN THE PRINT IS UNPLUGGED TO YOUR LIKING, YOU CAN RESUME PRINTING ON YOUR FINAL PAPER. DEPENDING ON THE WEATHER CONDITIONS, YOU MAY NEED TO REFRESH THE SCREENS LIKE THIS A FEW TIMES OR MORE. AFTER A FEW HOURS, WHEN THESE PRINTS ARE DRY, YOU'LL REPEAT THESE STEPS TO PRINT THE NEXT COLOR.

9) CLEAN UP

WHILE THE FIRST ROUND OF PRINTING IS DRYING, WASH OUT THE USED SCREEN. PULL OFF THE TAPE, SCRAPE OFF THE UNUSED INK, AND SPRAY OFF THE SCREEN. MAKE SURE YOUR SINK HAS A TRAP TO COLLECT THE INK RESIDUE OR THE PIPES CAN GET PLUGGED. ANOTHER OPTION IS TO USE A WATER-FILLED PLASTIC TUB AND LET THE INK DEBRIS SETTLE. THIS INK AND DIRT CAN BE SCOOPED OUT LATER AND THROWN AWAY, OR WAIT UNTIL THE INK DRIES – THE RESIDUE WILL BREAK OFF PRETTY EASILY AND CAN BE DISCARDED.

10) FOLD AND BIND

YOUR WORK OF ART IS ALMOST COMPLETE. USE SOMETHING LIKE A STAPLER (LONG ARM OR PAMPHLET STAPLER) OR SEWING MACHINE TO ATTACH THE COVER TO THE INSIDE PAGES. PRESTO, YOU HAVE YOUR AMAZING, SILK SCREEN-PRINTED ZINE! THIS IS JUST THE BEGINNING OF POSSIBILITIES FOR YOUR ARTWORK PROJECTS...

GOOD LUCK AND HAVE FUN!

IF YOU LIKE THE **LOOK** OF SCREEN-PRINTING, BUT DON'T HAVE THE SPACE OR THE MONEY FOR A **REAL** SCREEN PRINT SET-UP...

Let's PRINT GOCCO

BY Jonathan Bennett

CONSIDER THE **GOCCO** PROFESSIONAL-QUALITY HOME PRINTING KIT.

AT ABOUT THE SIZE OF A SHOEBOX, MOLDED IN DURABLE BLUE PLASTIC, THE GOCCO IS A SELF-CONTAINED MINI SCREEN PRINTING KIT.

I MEAN **REALLY** MINI! MAXIMUM PRINT AREA IS **4×6** INCHES.

NOT **TOO** SMALL FOR A DIGEST-SIZED BOOKLET COVER OR TO ADD SOME COLOR TO THAT BLACK & WHITE XEROX ZINE. TRY USING MULTIPLE SCREENS TO MAKE A BIGGER IMAGE.

SLIP

OKAY, BUT **HOW** DOES THE GOCCO WORK?

THE TRUTH IS, NO ONE **REALLY** KNOWS. ITS GOT SOMETHING TO DO WITH LIGHT, HEAT, AND CARBON. IT'S NOT REALLY IMPORTANT...

YOU JUST WORRY ABOUT WHAT YOU'RE GOING TO PRINT.

...

YOU'LL NEED TO MAKE THE "CARBON MASTER" USING A PHOTO-COPY MACHINE...

WHAP!

THOUGH, SOME LASER PRINTERS ARE COMPATIBLE.

SHHH...

I USE AN HP LASER JET 1300.

THE GOCCO USES ITS OWN SMALL INEXPENSIVE* AND DISPOSABLE SCREENS.

* PACK OF 5 FOR $12.

LOAD ONE OF THESE PRE-COATED SCREENS INTO YOUR PRESS ...

CAREFULLY PLACE YOUR LASER PRINT OR XEROX "MASTER" ON THE STICKY PRINT PAD WITH A BLANK BACKING SHEET.

LODGE TWO OF THE ODD YELLOW BULBS* INTO THE EXPOSURE HOOD AND SNAP THE HOOD INTO PLACE ATOP THE GOCCO.

* BOX OF 10 BULBS $12.

NOW, SHEILD YOUR EYES... LOOK **AWAY**... AND PRESS THE GOCCO FIRMLY SHUT. TWO AA BATTERIES EN-GORGE THE BULBS WITH ENOUGH POWER TO **BLAST** THE AFRO-WOUND FILAMENT WITHIN TO **DUST** IN A BLINDING **FLASH** OF WHITE LIGHT!

mmm... YOU SMELL THAT? YOUR SCREEN IS NOW EXPOSED. CAREFULLY DISPOSE OF THE SMOLDERING BULBS.

REMOVE THE SCREEN, AND USING TUBES OF GOCCO INK* APPLY COLOR TO THE OPEN AREAS OF YOUR IMAGE BENEATH THE TRANSPARENT FILM.

* $3 PER TUBE

ONE DISTINCT ADVANTAGE OF THE GOCCO OVER TRA-DITIONAL SCREEN PRINTING IS THE ABILITY TO PRINT MULTIPLE COLORS ON A SINGLE SCREEN.

STAMP

SQUEEGEE

THIN SELF-ADHESIVE "INK BLOCKING" FOAM STRIPS PREVENT UNWANTED COLOR MIXING. BUILD A BARRIER AROUND YOUR IMAGE TO KEEP INK FROM BEING WASTED.

WITH YOUR SCREEN BACK IN PLACE, YOU'RE READY TO **PRINT**. THE PRINT PAD IS JUST STICKY ENOUGH TO HOLD YOUR PAPER IN ONE PLACE. THAT'S A **BIG** HELP FOR MULTI-SCREEN REGISTRATION.

THE MOMENT OF **TRUTH**. PRESS THE HANDLE DOWN JUST HARD ENOUGH TO FEEL THE PRINT PAD PUSHING BACK...

OPEN IT UP, AND THERE IT IS. IT'S **WORKING**!

WHIP

NOW, JUST GOTTA KEEP AT IT... GET "IN THE ZONE". YOU ARE A MACHINE... YOU ARE A **FACTORY**.

... BUT, IS IT **ART**?

THE END

THE CUT 'N' CORRAL

→ Now that you have made all your copies it's TIME To start putting your books together,

You can have the copy shop cut down your pages or you can do it yourself using either a paper trimmer or a utility blade

THE CHOPPER!

(AS FAR AS PAPER TRIMMERS GO, THE SLIDING TRIMMERS ARE MUCH BETTER AND SAFER THAN the CHOPPING KIND.)

BE CAREFUL!

THE BLADE'S IN HERE,

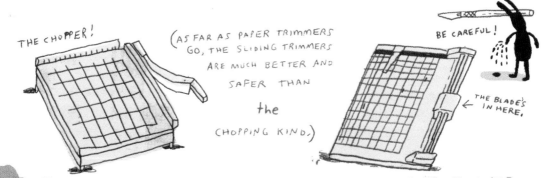

TIP → IF YOU'RE MAKING A LOT OF ZINES, YOU MAY WANT TO HAVE THE COPYSHOP CUT THEM FOR YOU. THEY USUALLY CHARGE PER CUT, AND THEIR SUPER CUTTER CAN CUT UP TO 100 PAGES AT ONCE.

DO THE MATH:
YOU: 1 CUT = 1-20 PAGES   THEM: 1 CUT = 100 PAGES
                                                (AND THEY CUT PERFECTLY.)

MODEL 20 SUPER CUT 3000

WARNING! WATCH YOUR HANDS,

8

For odd-sized zines you may have to make more
cuts depending on your zine format.

YOUR
→

THIS ZINE WAS SLIGHTLY SMALLER THAN A "MINI."
↓

① CUT YOUR PAGES.

CUT.

② TRIM it down,
(You can do this now or wait until the
book is together and trim at the end.)

TRIM ↓

TRIM ↓

TRIM ←

TRIM ←

TRIM ↓

STACK, FOLD, AND STAPLE.

③ ↓

(You can fold after
you staple. ON this
zine I wanted to make
sure the art lined up
so I folded first.)

④

⬦ ADD
FINISHING
TOUCHES.

☆ (IF YOU WAIT TILL THE END TO
TRIM YOUR ZINE, IT WILL LOOK
NICE AND CLEAN!)

JUST A BIT OFF
THE TOP, PLEASE.

NO
PROBLEM.

SURROUNDED BY PILES [...]

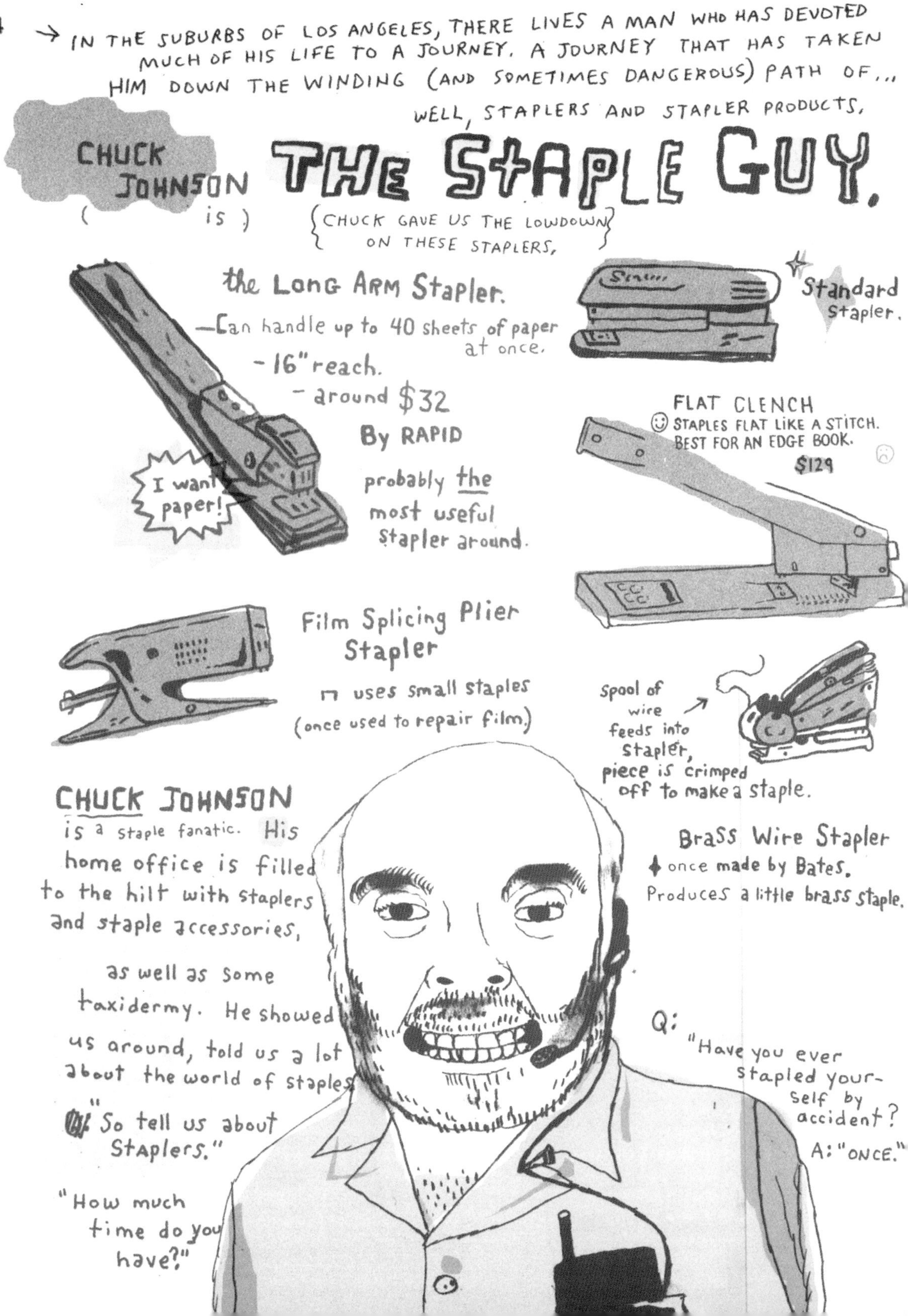
→ IN THE SUBURBS OF LOS ANGELES, THERE LIVES A MAN WHO HAS DEVOTED MUCH OF HIS LIFE TO A JOURNEY. A JOURNEY THAT HAS TAKEN HIM DOWN THE WINDING (AND SOMETIMES DANGEROUS) PATH OF... WELL, STAPLERS AND STAPLER PRODUCTS.
(CHUCK JOHNSON is) THE STAPLE GUY.
{CHUCK GAVE US THE LOWDOWN ON THESE STAPLERS.}
the LONG ARM Stapler.
—Can handle up to 40 sheets of paper at once.
- 16" reach.
- around $32
By RAPID
I want paper!
probably the most useful stapler around.
Standard Stapler.
FLAT CLENCH
☺ STAPLES FLAT LIKE A STITCH. BEST FOR AN EDGE BOOK.
$129
Film Splicing Plier Stapler
uses small staples (once used to repair film.)
Spool of wire feeds into stapler, piece is crimped off to make a staple.
Brass Wire Stapler
once made by Bates. Produces a little brass staple.
CHUCK JOHNSON is a staple fanatic. His home office is filled to the hilt with staplers and staple accessories,
as well as some taxidermy. He showed us around, told us a lot about the world of staples.
Q: "So tell us about Staplers."
"How much time do you have?"
Q: "Have you ever stapled yourself by accident?
A: "ONCE."

SWIVEL 210 by Etona
you can swivel the arm and staple in any direction.

This stapler, like the long-arm, is ideal for books where a standard stapler ~~coule~~ can't reach.
- uses standard staples
- about $35

wouldn't reach this way.

ROTATE

BLUE STRIPE

LOOK OUT
for these staplers at garage sales and thrift shops. Keep your eyes out for Toy Staplers like this one.

easy and lightning fast.

Etona makes a variety of colored staples.
- PINK - GOLD
  - GREEN - Blue
    - RED

LOOP STAPLE
→ your stapler would need a special driver. $58
- Great for 3 ring binders.

THE HOOK UP ZINE

- Electric
RAPID 105 Table Stapler
about $297

- Souther Salazar uses this stapler.

- RAPID 106 saddle stapler enables flat stapling. about $375

Foot Pedal Action.

STAPLER PEN
"ONE OF THE smallest STAPLERS"

mia familia!

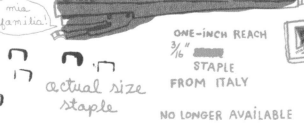

actual size staple

ONE-INCH REACH
3/16 "
STAPLE FROM ITALY

NO LONGER AVAILABLE

Max. Reach

I'LL RIP it out!!
Staple remover.

Unique Bindings

by: Saelee Oh

Here are some other ideas on how to bind your zines without stapling them in the traditional way...

(no offense, Stapler...)

hey... we staplers aren't so bad.

Office Supplies are good for binding zines!

brads

rubber bands

binder clips

clip a stack of paper

remove silver part

sewing isn't just for making clothes!

Different Materials

← ribbon

← yarn

dental floss

twine

shoe laces →

nest of thread, embroidery floss & raffia

The possibilities are endless!

Try: sewing your zine!

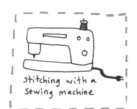

stitching with a sewing machine

Try sewing on the fold...

OR

Sew through all your pages on one side.

You can leave the ends as loose thread or cut it short.

(Many newer machines have decorative stitches).

handsewing with needle and thread

1.

2.

Use an awl (sharp tool for punching holes) to poke holes into the spine of your zine. then, thread a needle and weave the string in and out of each hole, going in one direction and then back the other direction. Tie two ends of string at end.

saddle stitch

1.

Put the thread through the needle and tie the end.

2.

Use an awl to punch 3 holes on the fold of the zine.

3.

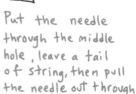

a →
b ←

Put the needle through the middle hole, leave a tail of string, then pull the needle out through the bottom hole.

4.

Thread the needle through the top hole.

5.

Pull the needle and thread out through the middle hole.

6.

Tie a bow with the two ends of the string and you're done!

so...

you've decided to make a 'zine

but what shape will it be?

SQUARE BINDING with power tools

by James McShane

Choosing:

is "digest-size" the only option?— no! a 'zine can be any size at all.

take a book off the shelf and turn it on it's end.

hey, it's made of many smaller signatures glued next to each other

maybe I could figure out how to do this?

paste-up:

paginating can be tricky—fold a sheet of paper in half three times. & paste your pages down in the following order:

flip

on the next signature, add 16 to each number to make pages 17-32 etc

tools & definitions:

"digest" refers to a 'zine the size of a sheet of paper folded in half.

a "signature" is a printed sheet that will be cut into multiple pages.

I use "hot glue" because it dries in minutes — instead of overnight.

a "jigsaw" is a woodworking tool used to make small, precise cuts.

stapling:

after the copies are made, each sheet is folded into 16ths and then stapled— so that the pages will stay together when the 'zine gets trimmed

rubber bands help keep the groups together

the cover:

hold your stapled signatures next to eachother. this will show you how much space to leave for the spine when you make the cover

squeeze

trim | back cover | spine | front cover | trim

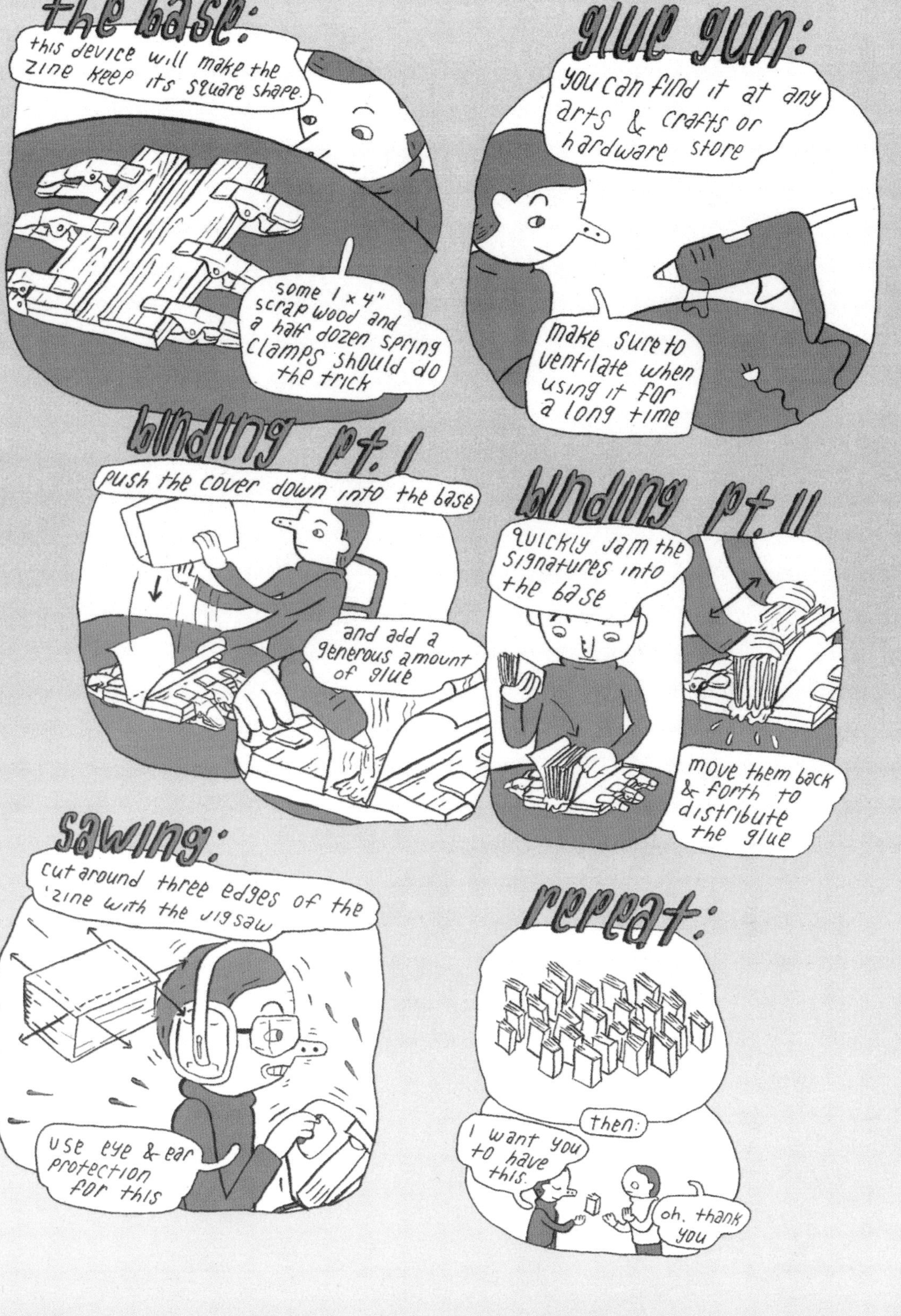
the base:
this device will make the zine keep its square shape.
some 1 x 4" scrap wood and a half dozen spring clamps should do the trick
glue gun:
you can find it at any arts & crafts or hardware store
make sure to ventilate when using it for a long time
binding pt. I
push the cover down into the base
and add a generous amount of glue
binding pt. II
quickly jam the signatures into the base
move them back & forth to distribute the glue
sawing:
cut around three edges of the 'zine with the jigsaw
use eye & ear protection for this
repeat:
then:
I want you to have this.
oh, thank you

5 gold-encrusted tips for getting it out there

Make it look rad ✦ your zine can be very home grown, or super slick; either way take the time to do it up right. Get some color on the cover. letterpress, silk-screen, do color copies, or use crayons and pens. Even just using a nice thick cardstock will make a difference.

postal guerrilla warfare ✦ Find out who's in charge and start mailing out those zines. Send them to distros, zines and websites that do reviews.

WISDOM

PEACE

Hey look, it's old man spoons

is there more?

when you send out your zines or comics make it clear what you want. Whether it's a review, ads for your zine, distribution, or to just strut your mad talents. Then do it all again. Send follow-up postcards or emails to the same and new contacts.

★ Get your own website up ★ so that if somebody in Pakistan wants to buy or trade they have a way to contact and check out your stuffs. Your site doesn't need to be super fancy, just a way for peeple to reach you.

★ comic and zine conventions are your friend. travel to as many zine and comic gigs as possible. this is a great way to sell and trade your zines, and best of all, make piles of new friends. Being at these shows is the best promotion I can think of. Book a table space, stand up, and be willing to say hi to new peeple.

★ you are your zine's sherpa ★ keep your zine with you at all times. Take copies and sell them at punk shows, bring them to coffee houses, ba-ring them everywhere you go. There is always someone new to share them with. Have fun and make rad zines. xoxo

Dwama
Spoons

MAKE CONTACT.

"come in, over."

"ROGER, ROGER?"

"GO AHEAD, ROGER. (IT'S M ROGE"

On the following pages are some samples of different ways people have listed contact information.

By including things like an e-mail, website, or snail mail address, you can let readers contact you for future issues, send trades, or simply write you a note. We see contact info all over zines: inside cover, back page, back of the zine, or in random places. Sometimes there is no name or contact information at all.

Some people like to make up a publishing name to zine under.

☆ This zine follows a traditional presentation of the publisher's information...

☆ This zine lists information all over the place. James doesn't stick to any set guidelines...

MAKE IT LOOK PRO.

the last lonely SATURDAY

by JORDAN CR

COPYRIGHT © 2000
BY JORDAN CRANE

FIRST EDITION: JULY 2000

Printed & Bound in Canada

the Last Lonely Saturday / by Jordan Crane
Crane, Jordan, 1973—
LIBRARY OF CONGRESS CATALOG CARD NUMBER: 99-095871
ISBN: 0-9571984-0-6

69 JOSEPHINE AVE. Floor One
SOMERVILLE, MA   02144
UNITED STATES
RED Book   www.beak.com/jordan

TITLE PAGE VERSO.   THE PAGE
FOLLOWING THE TITLE PAGE.
(CONTAINS PUBLISHING INFO
AS IN JORDAN CRANE'S "THE
LAST LONELY SATURDAY, "ABOVE.)

FOLLOW NO RULES.

november 2003

peck press
henrietter.net

Car

sleepy creatu

jamespmcshane @hotmail
www.fotolog.net/
James_m

FIND YOUR OWN WAY
TO LIST YOUR CONTACT
INFO. ■ PUT YOUR
PUBLISHING INFO IN
NONTRADITIONAL PLACES.

This is
JAMES MC SHANE'S
"CARMINE & DARNELL
& THE SLEEPY CREATURES

Rama Hughes keeps it simple and fun, listing his website and some questions for his readers. Jonathan Bennett includes his website and ordering information. He has an online account for people to make zine purchases directly over the web. Esther saves her information for the back cover.

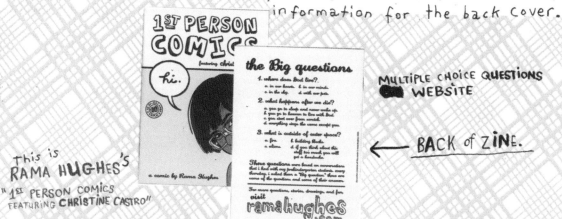

MULTIPLE CHOICE QUESTIONS
WEBSITE

← BACK of ZINE.

this is
RAMA HUGHES'S
"1ST PERSON COMICS
FEATURING CHRISTINE CASTRO"

THANK YOU
ORDERING INFO
ARTIST NAME
ADDRESS
WEB ACCOUNT INFO.
E-MAIL ADDRESS
WEBSITE

INSIDE BACK COVER.

this is
JONATHAN BENNETT'S
"PACK RAT"

WHERE MADE
WEBSITE
E-MAIL ADDRESS
COPYRIGHT DATE

BACK of ZINE. →

this is
ESTHER PEARL WATSON'S
"UNLOVABLE #3"

John Porcellino includes a short story.
Martin Cendreda includes a recipe, some recommended websites
& other zines to look for. Dave Kiersh lists CD ordering
information. What a cool idea!

TITLE OF ZINE
RECIPE FOR CANDY CANE BEVERAGE
COPYRIGHT DATE
NAME OF ARTIST
E-MAIL ADDRESS
WEBSITE
DATE
RECOMMENDED SITES AND ZINES

(nice guy!)

This is
MARTIN
CENDREDA'S
"DANG! #2"

INSIDE COVER!

WRITINGS
TITLE OF ZINE AND ISSUE
DATE PUBLISHED
PUBLISHER NAME
ADDRESS
SPECIAL THANKS

This is
JOHN PORCELLINO'S
"KING CAT COMICS
AND STORIES #55"

INSIDE COVER.

This is
DAVE KIERSH'S
"MY FAVORITE"

WORDS BY
PICTURES BY
COPYRIGHT DATE
WEBSITE
E-MAIL
CD ORDERING INFO

INSIDE BACK COVER.

PLACES TO LEAVE YOUR ZINE FOR FREE! FOR FUN!

any Public PLACE...

HIDE 'EM iN NEWSPAPERS.

WEDGE 'EM into LOCKERS.

LEAVE 'EM AT: the Doctor's Office

LEAVE 'EM AT:

MOViE HOUSES

LiBRARY

LAUNDRY mat

SUBWAY

on a nice PARK BENCH

ZINE

ARCADES

COFFEE SHOPS

THRiFT STORES

SODA Machines

READ ME.

TeLePHONE BOOTHS

COPY STORES

CAR WiNDshieLDS

the airplane

CONCERtS

PLACES where PEOPLE SiT

BuS StoPS

TiE 'EM TO HELiUM BALLOONS.

FaRMER's market

RECORD StoReS

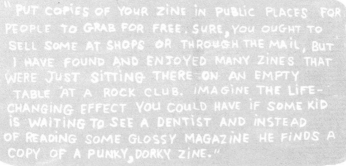

"PUT COPIES OF YOUR ZINE IN PUBLIC PLACES FOR PEOPLE TO GRAB FOR FREE. SURE, YOU OUGHT TO SELL SOME AT SHOPS OR THROUGH THE MAIL, BUT I HAVE FOUND AND ENJOYED MANY ZINES THAT WERE JUST SITTING THERE ON AN EMPTY TABLE AT A ROCK CLUB. IMAGINE THE LIFE-CHANGING EFFECT YOU COULD HAVE IF SOME KID IS WAITING TO SEE A DENTIST AND INSTEAD OF READING SOME GLOSSY MAGAZINE HE FINDS A COPY OF A PUNKY, DORKY ZINE."

JONATHAN BENNETT

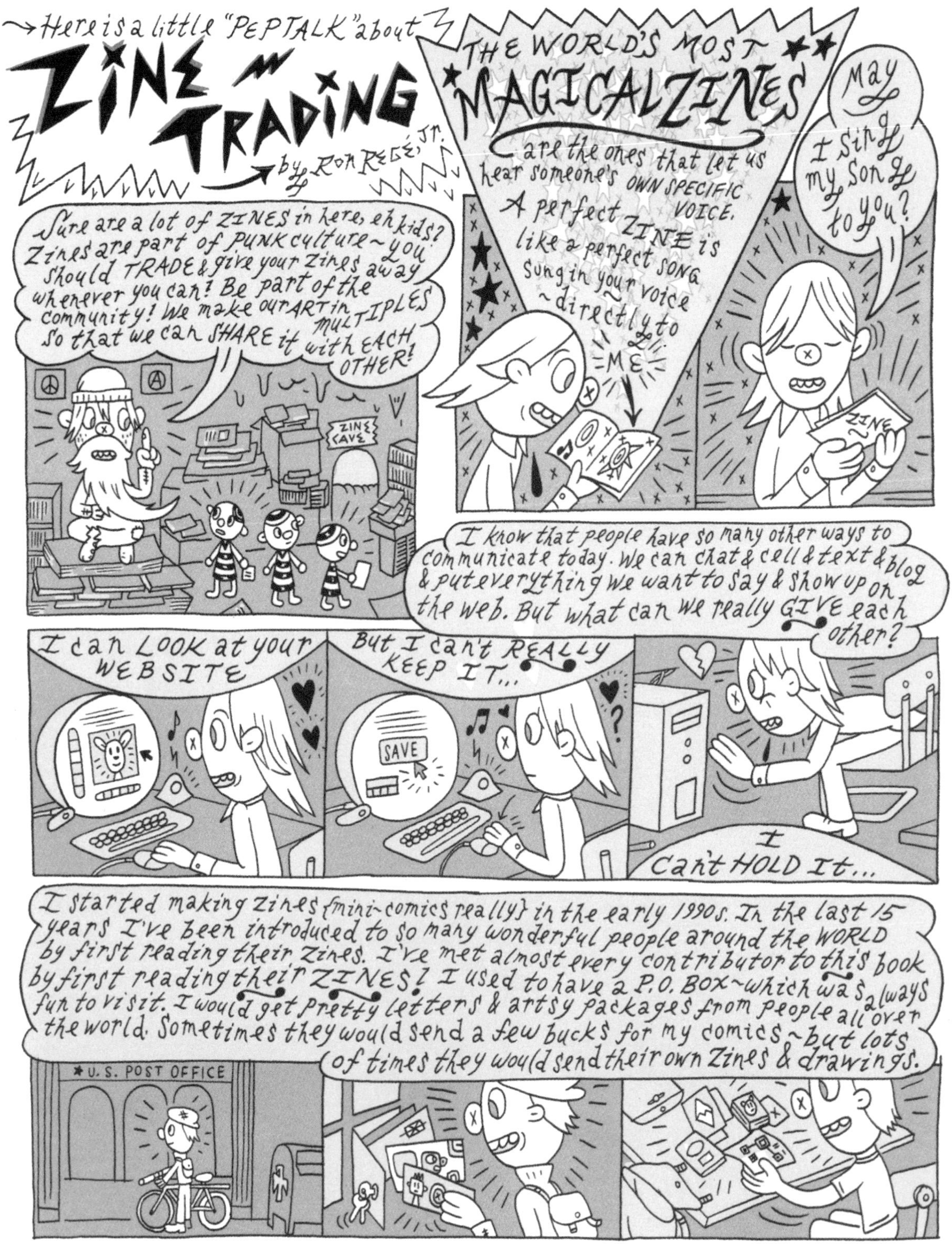
Here is a little "PEPTALK" about
ZINE TRADING
by RON REGÉ, JR.
THE WORLD'S MOST MAGICAL ZINES
are the ones that let us hear someone's OWN SPECIFIC VOICE.
A perfect ZINE is like a perfect SONG sung in your voice ~ directly to ME
May I sing my song to you?
Sure are a lot of ZINES in here, eh kids? Zines are part of PUNK culture ~ you should TRADE & give your zines away whenever you can! Be part of the community! We make our ART in MULTIPLES so that we can SHARE it with EACH OTHER!
ZINE CAVE
ZINE
I know that people have so many other ways to communicate today. We can chat & cell & text & blog & put everything we want to say & show up on the web. But what can we really GIVE each other?
I can LOOK at your WEBSITE
SAVE
But I can't REALLY KEEP IT...
I can't HOLD IT...
I started making zines {mini-comics really} in the early 1990s. In the last 15 years I've been introduced to so many wonderful people around the WORLD by first reading their zines. I've met almost every contributor to this book by first reading their ZINES! I used to have a P.O. BOX ~ which was always fun to visit. I would get pretty letters & artsy packages from people all over the world. Sometimes they would send a few bucks for my comics ~ but lots of times they would send their own zines & drawings.
U.S. POST OFFICE

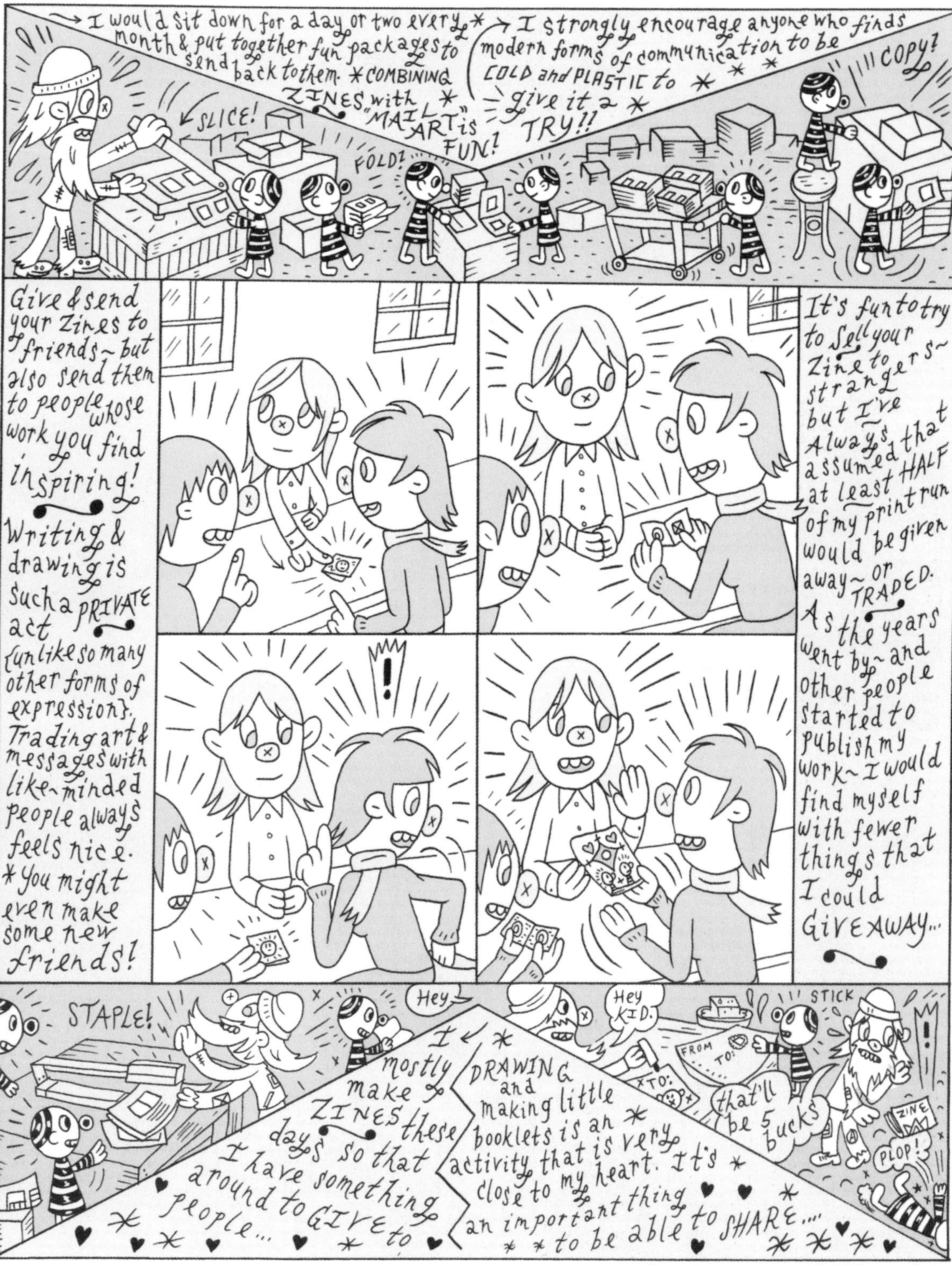
I would sit down for a day or two every month & put together fun packages to send back to them.
*COMBINING ZINES with "MAIL ART" is FUN!
SLICE!
FOLD!
I strongly encourage anyone who finds modern forms of communication to be COLD and PLASTIC to give it a TRY!!
COPY!
Give & send your Zines to friends~ but also send them to people whose work you find inspiring!
Writing & drawing is such a PRIVATE act {unlike so many other forms of expression}. Trading art & messages with like-minded people always feels nice. *You might even make some new friends!
It's fun to try to sell your Zine to strangers~ but I've always assumed that at least HALF of my print run would be given away~ or TRADED.
As the years went by~ and other people started to publish my work~ I would find myself with fewer things that I could GIVEAWAY...
STAPLE!
Hey
Hey KID.
STICK
FROM
TO:
TO:
that'll be 5 bucks
ZINE
PLOP!
I mostly make ZINES these days so that I have something around to GIVE to people...
DRAWING and making little booklets is an activity that is very close to my heart. It's an important thing to be able to SHARE....

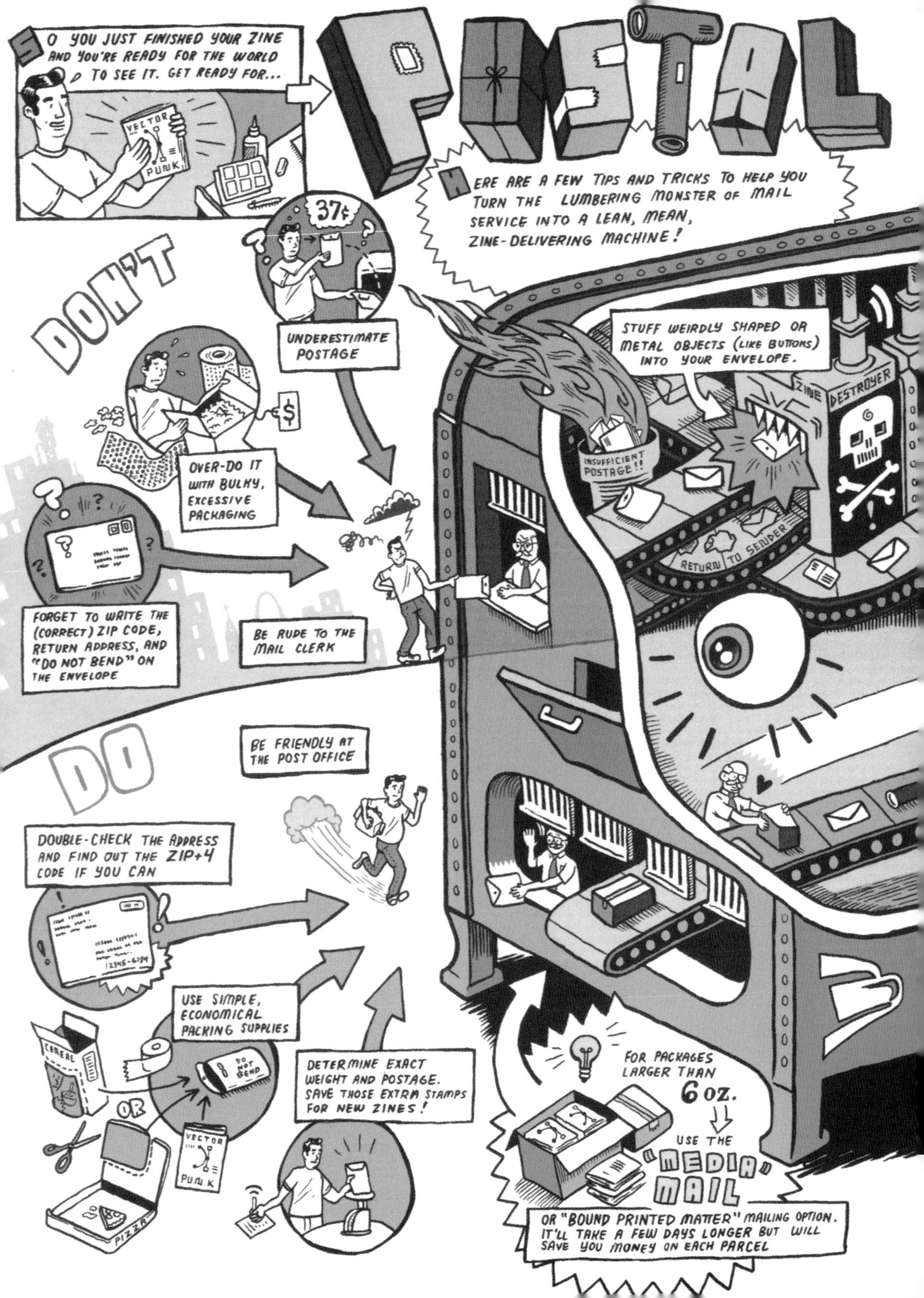
SO YOU JUST FINISHED YOUR ZINE AND YOU'RE READY FOR THE WORLD TO SEE IT. GET READY FOR...
POSTAL
VECTOR PUNK
HERE ARE A FEW TIPS AND TRICKS TO HELP YOU TURN THE LUMBERING MONSTER OF MAIL SERVICE INTO A LEAN, MEAN, ZINE-DELIVERING MACHINE!
DON'T
37¢
UNDERESTIMATE POSTAGE
OVER-DO IT WITH BULKY, EXCESSIVE PACKAGING
FORGET TO WRITE THE (CORRECT) ZIP CODE, RETURN ADDRESS, AND "DO NOT BEND" ON THE ENVELOPE
BE RUDE TO THE MAIL CLERK
STUFF WEIRDLY SHAPED OR METAL OBJECTS (LIKE BUTTONS) INTO YOUR ENVELOPE.
INSUFFICIENT POSTAGE!!
ZINE DESTROYER
RETURN TO SENDER
DO
BE FRIENDLY AT THE POST OFFICE
DOUBLE-CHECK THE ADDRESS AND FIND OUT THE ZIP+4 CODE IF YOU CAN
12345-6789
USE SIMPLE, ECONOMICAL PACKING SUPPLIES
CEREAL
OR
DO NOT BEND
PIZZA
DETERMINE EXACT WEIGHT AND POSTAGE. SAVE THOSE EXTRA STAMPS FOR NEW ZINES!
FOR PACKAGES LARGER THAN 6 OZ.
USE THE "MEDIA" MAIL
OR "BOUND PRINTED MATTER" MAILING OPTION. IT'LL TAKE A FEW DAYS LONGER BUT WILL SAVE YOU MONEY ON EACH PARCEL

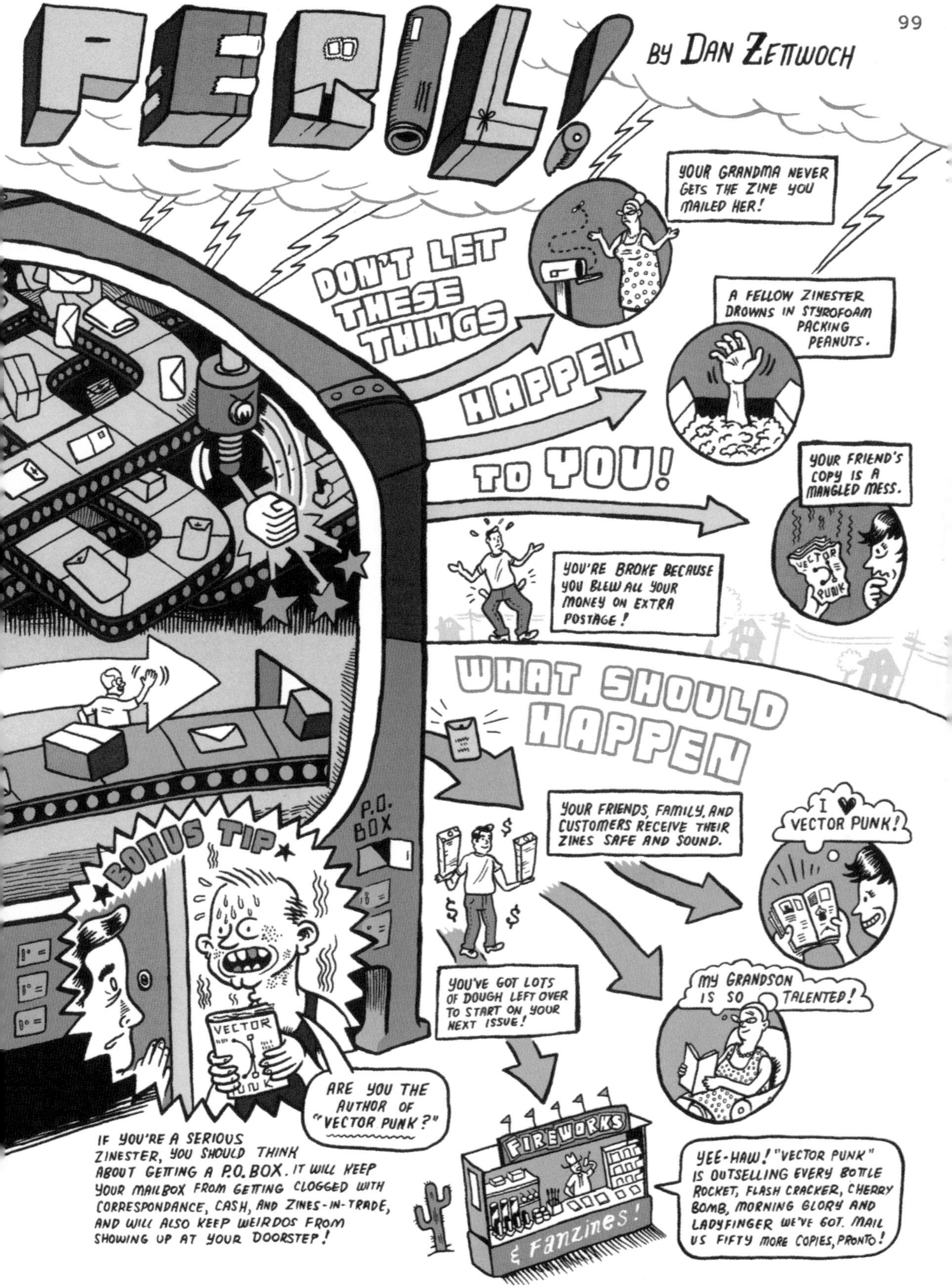
PERIL!
BY DAN ZETTWOCH
DON'T LET THESE THINGS HAPPEN TO YOU!
YOUR GRANDMA NEVER GETS THE ZINE YOU MAILED HER!
A FELLOW ZINESTER DROWNS IN STYROFOAM PACKING PEANUTS.
YOUR FRIEND'S COPY IS A MANGLED MESS.
VECTOR PUNK
YOU'RE BROKE BECAUSE YOU BLEW ALL YOUR MONEY ON EXTRA POSTAGE!
WHAT SHOULD HAPPEN
YOUR FRIENDS, FAMILY, AND CUSTOMERS RECEIVE THEIR ZINES SAFE AND SOUND.
I ♥ VECTOR PUNK!
YOU'VE GOT LOTS OF DOUGH LEFT OVER TO START ON YOUR NEXT ISSUE!
MY GRANDSON IS SO TALENTED!
FIREWORKS
& Fanzines!
YEE-HAW! "VECTOR PUNK" IS OUTSELLING EVERY BOTTLE ROCKET, FLASH CRACKER, CHERRY BOMB, MORNING GLORY AND LADYFINGER WE'VE GOT. MAIL US FIFTY MORE COPIES, PRONTO!
P.O. BOX
BONUS TIP
VECTOR PUNK
ARE YOU THE AUTHOR OF "VECTOR PUNK?"
IF YOU'RE A SERIOUS ZINESTER, YOU SHOULD THINK ABOUT GETTING A P.O. BOX. IT WILL KEEP YOUR MAILBOX FROM GETTING CLOGGED WITH CORRESPONDANCE, CASH, AND ZINES-IN-TRADE, AND WILL ALSO KEEP WEIRDOS FROM SHOWING UP AT YOUR DOORSTEP!

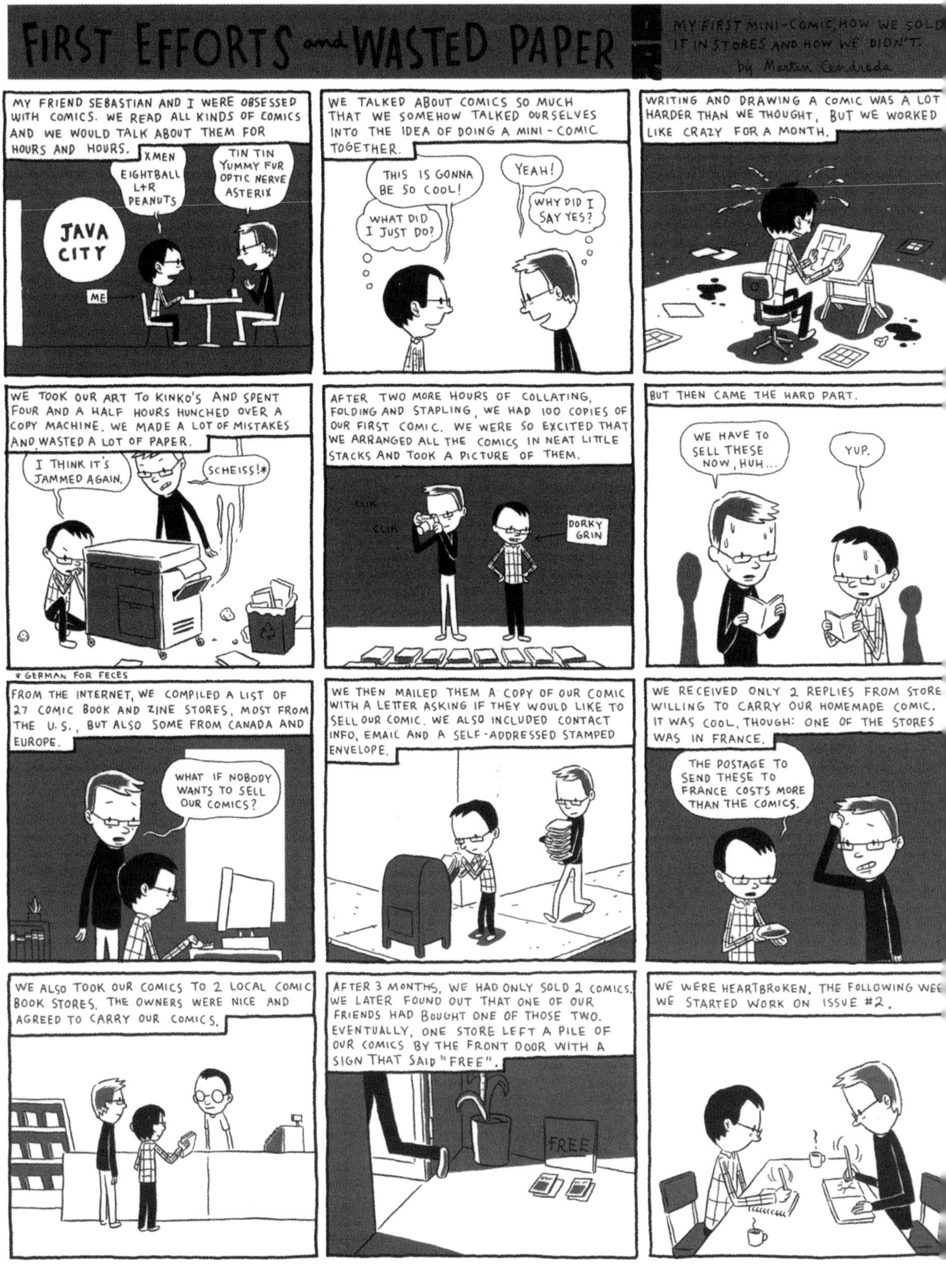
FIRST EFFORTS and WASTED PAPER
MY FIRST MINI-COMIC, HOW WE SOLD IT IN STORES AND HOW WE DIDN'T.
by Martin Cendreda
MY FRIEND SEBASTIAN AND I WERE OBSESSED WITH COMICS. WE READ ALL KINDS OF COMICS AND WE WOULD TALK ABOUT THEM FOR HOURS AND HOURS.
XMEN EIGHTBALL L+R PEANUTS
TIN TIN YUMMY FUR OPTIC NERVE ASTERIX
JAVA CITY
ME
WE TALKED ABOUT COMICS SO MUCH THAT WE SOMEHOW TALKED OURSELVES INTO THE IDEA OF DOING A MINI-COMIC TOGETHER.
THIS IS GONNA BE SO COOL!
WHAT DID I JUST DO?
YEAH!
WHY DID I SAY YES?
WRITING AND DRAWING A COMIC WAS A LOT HARDER THAN WE THOUGHT, BUT WE WORKED LIKE CRAZY FOR A MONTH.
WE TOOK OUR ART TO KINKO'S AND SPENT FOUR AND A HALF HOURS HUNCHED OVER A COPY MACHINE. WE MADE A LOT OF MISTAKES AND WASTED A LOT OF PAPER.
I THINK IT'S JAMMED AGAIN.
SCHEISS!*
* GERMAN FOR FECES
AFTER TWO MORE HOURS OF COLLATING, FOLDING AND STAPLING, WE HAD 100 COPIES OF OUR FIRST COMIC. WE WERE SO EXCITED THAT WE ARRANGED ALL THE COMICS IN NEAT LITTLE STACKS AND TOOK A PICTURE OF THEM.
CLIK
CLIK
DORKY GRIN
BUT THEN CAME THE HARD PART.
WE HAVE TO SELL THESE NOW, HUH...
YUP.
FROM THE INTERNET, WE COMPILED A LIST OF 27 COMIC BOOK AND ZINE STORES, MOST FROM THE U.S., BUT ALSO SOME FROM CANADA AND EUROPE.
WHAT IF NOBODY WANTS TO SELL OUR COMICS?
WE THEN MAILED THEM A COPY OF OUR COMIC WITH A LETTER ASKING IF THEY WOULD LIKE TO SELL OUR COMIC. WE ALSO INCLUDED CONTACT INFO, EMAIL AND A SELF-ADDRESSED STAMPED ENVELOPE.
WE RECEIVED ONLY 2 REPLIES FROM STORES WILLING TO CARRY OUR HOMEMADE COMIC. IT WAS COOL, THOUGH: ONE OF THE STORES WAS IN FRANCE.
THE POSTAGE TO SEND THESE TO FRANCE COSTS MORE THAN THE COMICS.
WE ALSO TOOK OUR COMICS TO 2 LOCAL COMIC BOOK STORES. THE OWNERS WERE NICE AND AGREED TO CARRY OUR COMICS.
AFTER 3 MONTHS, WE HAD ONLY SOLD 2 COMICS. WE LATER FOUND OUT THAT ONE OF OUR FRIENDS HAD BOUGHT ONE OF THOSE TWO. EVENTUALLY, ONE STORE LEFT A PILE OF OUR COMICS BY THE FRONT DOOR WITH A SIGN THAT SAID "FREE".
FREE
WE WERE HEARTBROKEN. THE FOLLOWING WEEK WE STARTED WORK ON ISSUE #2.

WHERE TO SHOP
{ AND DROP. }

33 1/3 Books
1200 N. Alvarado Blvd.
~~xxxxxxxxxxx~~
Echo Park, CA 90026

major support.

Atomic Books
1100 W. 36th Street
Baltimore, MD 21211
(410)662-4444
www.atomicbooks.com

Big Brain Comics
1027 Washington Ave. S.
Minneapolis, MN 55415
(612)338-4390 e-mail bigbrain@visi.com
www.avs-inc.com/bbc.jpg

Boxcar Books
310a S. Washington
Bloomington, IN
(812)339-8710
www.boxcarbooks.org
boxcar@boxcarbooks.org

← *MICHAEL DRIVAS*

Cinders Gallery
103 Havemeyer Street
Brooklyn, NY 11211
(718)388-2311
stocinders@earthlink.net

Artist-run gallery and store
in Williamsburg.

Comic Relief
2026 Shattuck Ave.
Berkeley, CA 94704
(510)843-5002

Confounded Books
315 Pine Street
Seattle, WA 98122
(206)382-3376

small but awesome.

in it for the long haul.

Giant Robot Store
2015 Sawtelle Blvd.
Los Angeles, CA 90025
(310)478-1819
www.giantrobot.com

GRNY
437 E. 9th St.
New York, NY 10009
(212)674-GRNY
www.GRNY.net

GRSF
622 Shrader St.
San Francisco, CA 94117
(415)876-GRSF.
www.gr-sf.com

Peter Birkemoe

The Beguiling
601 Markham Street
Toronto, Ontario
Canada M6G 2L7
(416)533-9168
www.beguiling.com

Junc Gallery
4017 Sunset Blvd.
Los Angeles, CA 90029
(626)298-3014
www.juncgallery.com

⭐ *MIKE KELLEY!*

good, honest.

Needles+Pens
483 14th St.
San Francisco, CA 94103
www.needles-pens.com
(415)255-1534

raddest for zines

Other Music
15 E. 4th St.
New York, NY 10003
(212) 477-8150

Page 45
9 Market St.
Nottingham NG1 6HY
TEL:(0115)9508045
page45.com

← *ENGLAND*

Quimby's Bookstore
1854 W. North Ave.
Chicago, Il 60622
(773)342-0910

devoted to independent books, zines, minicomics.

Q Is For Choir Cooperative
2510 SE Clinton Street
Portland, OR 97202
(503)235-9678

Jeff Mason has a list of
Indy-Friendly Bookstores .
www.indyworld.com/comics/stores.html

IPRC or Independent Publishing
Resource Center
917 SW Oak Street, Suite 218
Portland, OR 97205
(503)827-0249

www.iprc.org/about.php

Resources and tools for creation
of Indie published media and art.
Nonprofit Organization.

Meltdown Comics
7522 Sunset Blvd
Los Angeles, CA 90046
(323)851-7223
www.meltcomics.com
e-mail staff@meltcomics.com

The Million Year Picnic
99 Mount Auburn Street
Cambridge, MA 02138
(617)492-6763

Tony Davis is theowner and he's
a really nice guy. --Allison Cole

Printed Matter
535 W. 22nd St.
New York, NY 10011
(212) 925-0325
printedmatter.org

REading Frenzy
921 SW Oak STreet
Portland, OR 97205
(503)274-1449
www.readingfrenzy.com

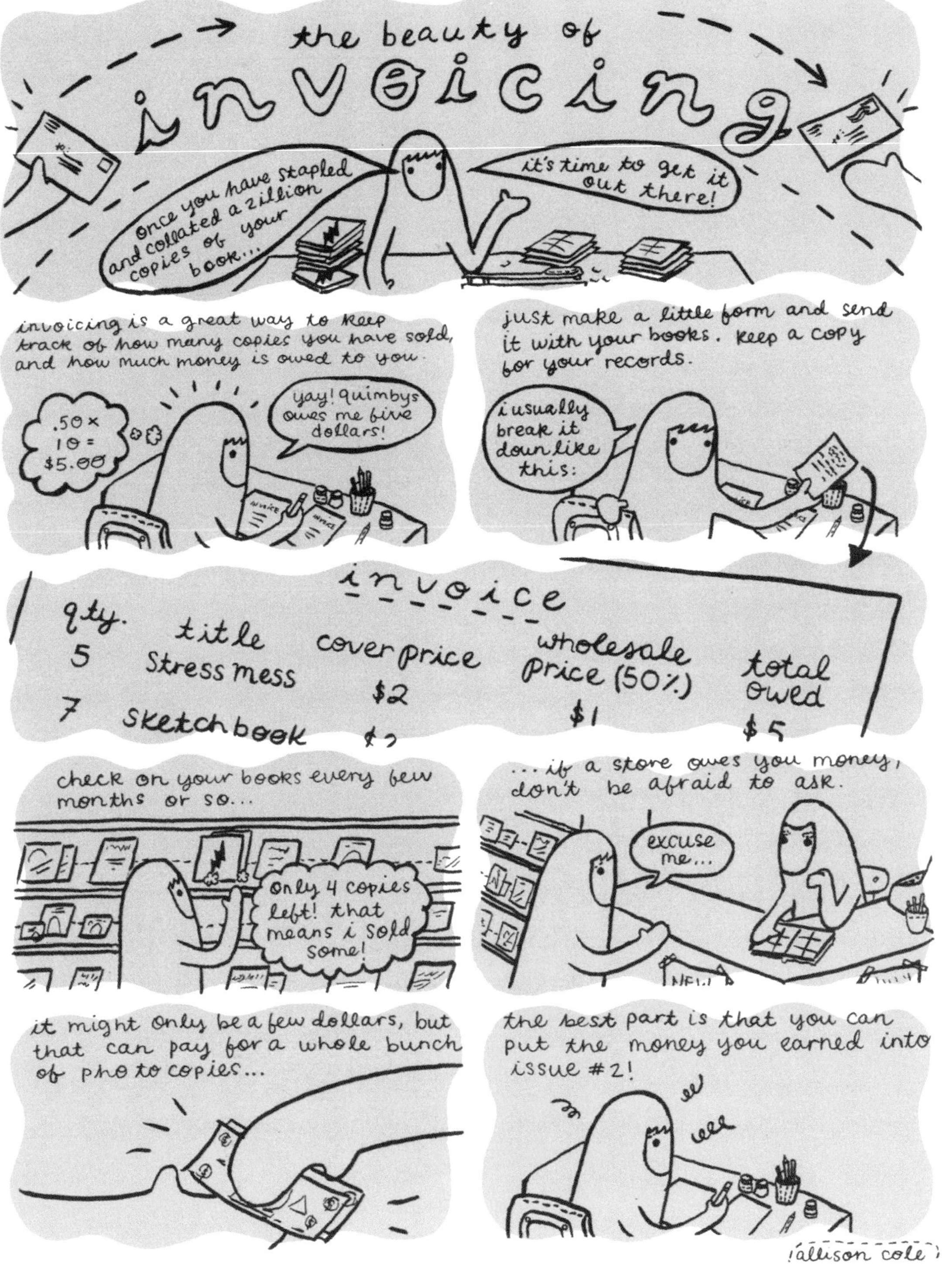
the beauty of
invoicing
once you have stapled and collated a zillion copies of your book...
it's time to get it out there!
invoicing is a great way to keep track of how many copies you have sold, and how much money is owed to you.
.50 × 10 = $5.00
yay! quimbys owes me five dollars!
just make a little form and send it with your books. keep a copy for your records.
i usually break it down like this:
invoice
qty.
title
cover price
wholesale price (50%)
total owed
5
Stress mess
$2
$1
$5
7
sketchbook
check on your books every few months or so...
Only 4 copies left! that means i sold some!
...if a store owes you money, don't be afraid to ask.
excuse me...
it might only be a few dollars, but that can pay for a whole bunch of photocopies...
the best part is that you can put the money you earned into issue #2!
allison cole

{ DISTRO }

⭐ Distros →

(short for zine distributors) are places that sell zines and mini-comics. Some distros, like Quimby's in Chicago, have physical store locations as well as virtual online shops to visit. Others, like USS CATASROPH and POOPSHEET SHOP are online only.

There are also small press book publishers/distributors like LAST GASP.

ON CONSIGNMENT

Some stores don't have the cash to buy your zines upfront, or they don't want to risk losing money on zines that might not sell.

Some places ask for a free "sample copy." If a distro places an order be sure to send your zines out right away. Don't sit on the order for a year so the Distro can't remember who you are.

Payment is usually 50% of the retail price payable IF and AFTER the zine sells. Then you get a check in the mail.

Unfortunately, some places are not reputable, forget you, keep bad records, go out of business, or come up with other lame excuses not to mail out your check.

DISTROS MOVE AND GO DEFUNCT, SO CHECK ONLINE FOR THE LATEST INFO. AND LOCATIONS.

Here's how it might go down: An online distro e-mails and want samples. We mail out & Unlovable #1 that I sell for $5 retail(customer price) and Bad Ass that Mark sells for $2 retail. The online distro orders 5 Unlovables and 5 Bad Asses...so that's about $35 (customer price) retail. But Mark and I don't get mailed a check until they all sell.

That is if all goes smoothly.

WHOLESALE

Here's another way it might go down (that we like better): Mark and I fill a shoe box with our mini-comics and drive around town to our favorite comic/book stores, and show the owner our box of zines right there on the spot. The store owner buys 5 Unlovables and 5 Bad Asses ...remember that retails for a total of $35 and the owner hands over the wholesale price right there on the spot. We walk out with $17.50 and spend it right away!

GOOD PLACE TO READ MORE ABOUT ZINE DISTRIBUTION IS CHIP ROWE'S ZINEBOOK.COM
THERE ARE INTERVIEWS AND LINKS TO DISTRIBUTORS.

ZINE RESOURCES!

BOOKS.

The World of Zines, A Guide to the Independent Magazine REvolution
by Mike Gunderloy and CAri Goldberg (Penguin Books 1992)

Stolen Sharpie Revolution by Alex Wrekk
Microcosm PUblsihing   www.microcosmpublshing.com

The Book of Zines, Edited by Chip Rowe (Owl Books, A Division of Henry Holt, 1997)

Notes from Underground, and the Politics of Alternative Culture, by Stephen Duncombe
(Verso of London, 1997)

Zine Scene, The Do It Yourself Guide to Zines, by Francesca Lia Block & Hilary Carlip
(Girl Press, 1998)

?r   From Girls to Grrrlz, A History of Comics from Teens to Zines, by Tina Robbins
(Chronicle 1999)

Fucked Up + Photocopied, Instant Art of the Punk Rock Movement, by Bryan Ray   Turcotte
& Christopher T. Miller (Gingko Press Inc.)

HOW-TOS.

A Guide to REproduction
Primer on Xerography, silkscreening
and Offset   Printing.
          www.reddingk.com/reproguide.pdf
by Ron Regé,Jr.,Dave Choe, Brian Ralph,
Jordan Crane.

Zinebook
Chip Rowe's online
resources on how to make,
distribute, and print zines.
Zinebook.com

Zine World:A REader's Guide to the Underground Press
www.undergroundpress.org
P.O. Box 330156
Murfreesboro, TN 37133

Links to store, distros, lots more
plus will review your zine.

Zine CONVENTIONS.

Alternative Press Expo
www.comic-con.org

Philadelphia Zine Fest
geocities.com/phillyzinefest

Small Press ExPo (SPX)
www. spxpo.com

MOCCA Arts Festival
www.moccany.org

Portland Zine Symposium
www.pdxzines.com

WHERE TO SEND 'EM.

Zine Street
Lists Distros, Stores, Libraries
www.zinestreet.com

U.S.S. Catastrophe
Online Distro for Mini Comics
www.usscatastrophe.com

apply for a comic book
self-publishing grant !
XERIC FOUNDATION
PMB 214
351 Pleasant St.
Northampton, Massachusetts
01060

413/585-0671

www.xericfoundation.com

project MOBILIVRE BOOKMOBILE PROJECT
c/o Space 1026
1026 Arch Street
Philadelphia, PA 19107

Vintage Airstream touring
exhibition of artist books,
zines, and independent
publications.

Submit zines with Application
from website:
www.mobilivre.org

Now that you have all those copies don't let them sit in
your closet under a pile of clothes. You can rent a table
at alternative press conventions and sell your zines for
a couple of bucks apiece. You can send them to be reviewed in
in other zines and magazines, or set up a website devoted
to distributing your zine. Mail copies to your favorite artists
and to zine libraries. Give a few to your friends, family, and
maybe some old guy at the post office. Don't be shy, send them
out into the world!

SLOW SALES and ACCIDENTAL DINNERS

MY FRIEND JOHN AND I DECIDED TO GET A TABLE AT A CONVENTION TO SELL OUR COMICS. OUR TABLE ENDED UP BEING WAY DEEP IN THE BACK OF THE HALL.

ALL THE ACTION

TUMBLE-WEED

WE DIDN'T KNOW A SINGLE PERSON THERE, AND WITH OUR COMICS OUT ON THE TABLE FOR ALL TO JUDGE, WE FELT ABSOLUTELY NAKED.

WE GOT TO TALKING TO OUR NEIGHBORS, WHO WERE ALSO FIRST-TIME SELLERS. WE QUICKLY BONDED OVER OUR SHARED ANXIETIES

IT'S SO NERVE-WRACKING, ISN'T IT?!

YEAH!

ABOUT AN HOUR PASSED BEFORE PEOPLE ACTUALLY STOPPED AT OUR TABLE. SOME BOUGHT STUFF, SOME DIDN'T.

AT THE END OF THE FIRST DAY, JOHN AND I WENT TO HAVE DINNER WITH HIS FRIENDS, BUT SOMEHOW WE GOT SEPERATED FROM THEM.

SHIT. WHAT SHOULD WE DO NOW?

LUCKILY, RON AND BRIAN FROM HIGHWATER BOOKS NOTICED HOW LOST AND CONFUSED WE LOOKED, AND ASKED US IF WE WANTED TO HAVE DINNER WITH THEM AND THE REST OF THE HIGHWATER CREW.

HEY, YOU WANNA HAVE DINNER WITH US?

SURE!!

JOHN AND I WERE SHY, AND DIDN'T TALK MUCH. EVERYONE ELSE SHARED FUNNY STORIES AND ANECTDOTES ABOUT THEIR EXPERIENCES IN THE COMIC WORLD.

REMEMBER WHEN WE CRASHED AT THAT WEIRD GUY'S HOUSE...

OR HOW ABOUT THE TIME WE HAD TO DRIVE TO CANADA TO GET YOUR BOOKS.

WHAT THE HECK IS A PUPUSA?

LATER THAT NIGHT, AS JOHN AND I WERE GOING TO SLEEP, WE COULDN'T STOP TALKING ABOUT OUR "ACCIDENTAL" DINNER.

I CAN'T BELIEVE WE HAD DINNER WITH THE HIGHWATER GUYS!

SO CRAZY HUH!

I KNOW!

I KNOW!!

THE SECOND DAY OF THE CONVENTION WAS MUCH LIKE THE FIRST.

HOW COME SOME PEOPLE LOOK AT OUR COMICS FOR A LONG TIME, BUT THEN THEY LEAVE WITHOUT BUYING ANYTHING?!!

YEAH! OR HOW SOME PEOPLE BUY EVERYTHING WITHOUT EVEN LOOKING INSIDE!

DIDN'T BUY

AS THE CONVENTION DREW TO A CLOSE, WE ENDED UP TRADING COMICS WITH A LOT OF OTHER ARTISTS, MANY OF WHOM WERE FIRST-TIMERS LIKE US.

SCREW KINKO'S! YOU SHOULD USE MINUTEMAN!

THANKS!

THAT WEEKEND, WE DIDN'T SELL VERY MANY COMICS, BUT WE HAD MADE SOME FRIENDS WHO, LIKE US, WERE JUST STARTING OUT. AND WE HAD DINNER WITH SOME ARTISTS WHOSE WORK WE HAD READ AND ADMIRED.

THE DRIVE HOME TO L.A. WAS LONG AND EXHAUSTING. WE DROVE FOR 6 HOURS. OUR BODIES WERE TIRED AND ACHEY. BUT OUR MINDS WERE GOING A MILE A MINUTE.

ZiNE LiBRARiES

Send your zine to one of the many zine libraries that will protect and preserve your self-published work.

Your zine will be seen over and over by different people who might not have access to your super-limited print run.

* cool bonus * you get friendly thank-notes sometimes with personalized art!

Richard Hugo House
Zine ARchive Project
1634 Eleventh Ave.
Seattle, Washington
98122

PERSONAL THANK-YOU LETTER

Denver Zine Library
111 W. Archer Pl.
Denver, Colorado
80223

SENT THANK-YOU in HAND-MADE ENVELOPE + VINYL STICKERS

LIKES BAY AREA ZINES

San Francisco
Public Library
Little Magazine
Collection

100 Larkin St.
San Francisco, California
94102

BOOKWORM
ZINEWORM SAYS:

WORM ZINE

THANK YOU.

San Diego State U.
Special Collections
5500 Campanile Dr.
San Diego, Californ
92182-8050

Urbana-Champaign
Independent Media Center
218 West Main St.
Urbana, Illinois 61801

FACTSHEET 5'S HOMETOWN

New York State Library
Manuscripts and
Special Collections
Albany, NY 12230

" LARGEST ZINE COLLECTION IN CENTRAL ILLINOIS "

Independent Publishing
Resource Center
917 SW Oak St. #218

Portland, Oregon
97205

FRIENDLY PLACE TO LOOK AT ZINES

Salt Lake City
Public Library
209 E. 500 South
Salt Lake City, Utah
84111

THEY HAVE A ZINE-FRIENDLY WEBSITE TOO!

(This is a short list... ask friends and look on line for zine libraries and archives in your neighborhood.)

⸖ GLOSSARY. ⸘

Binding- fastening your zine pages together

Collating- gathering the pages of your zine in order

Co-Op -Cooperative, working together

Copyright - Ownership of writings, drawings, photos granted by law during a   set amount of time for protection of reproduction, sales and production.

DPI-dots per inch.

Distro-Distributor who sells your zines to stores and customers for a percentage of the profits.

Double-Up - having two zine pages on one sheet of paper

Factsheet Five-zine started by Mike Gunderloy in the 1980 s reviewed zines.

Four-Up- having four zine pages on one sheet of paper

Full Bleed- going to the edge of the paper

High Contrast, - striking difference in black-and-white tone

Independent or Indy-Not connected or related to any company.

Invoice-a list of zines sold, quantities, price, your address that you give to a distro or store; your bill

Mastercopy-your"original" art and text that you make Copies from

Offset Printer- professional printer who uses special inks(PMS Colors) on rubber-covered rollers   transferred to paper.

Original-same as your Mastercopy , what your reproductions are made from.

PMS color- Pantone Matching System used by offset printers.
www.pantone.com

Paginating-   arrangement and numbering of the pages of your zine.

Pound- Paper   weight, the thickness of a sheet of paper.

Publication Name-name of your zine

Review- someone reading your zine and summerizing what it is about and giving their opinion (good or bad).

Silk Screening-using a silk fabric for a printing screen,ink is pushed through the screen and imprinted onto paper.

Signatures- a section of a zine that is bound by itself and will later be bound with a group of identical-size sections of the zine.

Submissions- mailing a copy of your zine to a Distro, Zine Library for consideration, donation or review.

Table Space- Space rented at a zine fair, convention, etc.

Toner- Carbon dust that is printed onto paper from the photocopy machine

Trades,- exchanging your zine for someone else's

Zine Library- Place that houses zines that were donated

Zine Convention, - a place where people who make their own books, zines, products, sell . Independently published goods

JONATHAN BENNETT

WORKS AT ST. MARTIN'S PRESS BY DAY AND BY NIGHT CREATES WONDERFULLY MASTERED GOCCO PRINTED MINI-COMICS. HIS COMICS INCLUDE ESOTERIC TALES, RAT PACK, AND TORRENTIAL.

SMALLESTSOUND.COM

PETER HAMLIN

HAS CREATED BEAUTIFUL SILKSCREEN PRINTED ZINES, INCLUDING TINY LITTLE BITS, AND E.R.O.E.I. HE HAS ILLUSTRATED FOR THE NEW YORKER, LEGO, SONY MUSIC AND OTHERS.

HAMBOT.COM

LITTLE TINY BITS
P. Hamlin
VOLUME 1

SHANE PATRICK BOYLE

LIVES IN HOUSTON, TEXAS, WHERE HE HAS BEEN WRITING, DRAWING, AND SELF-PUBLISHING SINCE HIGH SCHOOL. HE PUBLISHES AN ONGOING ZINE TITLED SHANE AND IS THE FOUNDER/PRESIDENT OF THE HOUSTON AREA COMICS SOCIETY.

LAURIE HENZEL

IS THE CREATIVE DIRECTOR AND PUBLISHER OF BUST, A MAGAZINE "FOR WOMEN WITH SOMETHING TO GET OFF THEIR CHESTS." BEGUN IN 1993 AS A PHOTOCOPIED ZINE, IT NOW HAS A CIRCULATION OF OVER 81,000.

BUST.COM

BEN BUSH

WAS LUCKY ENOUGH TO GROW UP IN A HOME WITH A COPY MACHINE, WHICH FACILITATED SOME EARLY FORAYS INTO THE WORLD OF ZINES. HIS WRITING HAS APPEARED IN XLR8R, ALTERNET, BAY GUARDIAN, BITCH MAGAZINE AND TORONTO'S FLEDGLING LITERARY MAGAZINE THE SHORE.

CHUCK JOHNSON

HAS BEEN REPAIRING STAPLERS SINCE 1974. FROM ZINE-MAKERS IN CALIFORNIA TO COMIC SHOPS IN TORONTO, CHUCK HAS BEEN THE ONE TO CALL FOR PROFESSIONAL STAPLER PRODUCTS AND REPAIR.

JOHNSONSTAPLER.COM

MARTIN CENDREDA

IS A CARTOONIST/ANIMATOR LIVING IN L.A. HIS COMIC DANG! WAS PUBLISHED BY TOP SHELF COMICS. GIANT ROBOT PUBLISHED HIS BOOK, BARE FOOT RIOT.

ZURLKROBOT.COM

DAVE KIERSH

HAS WORKED AS A JUNIOR HIGH SCHOOL TEACHER AND LIBRARIAN. HE HAS CREATED MANY MINI-COMICS INCLUDING MY FAVORITE, GREATEST HITS, THE SERIES DIRTBAG, AND LAST CRY FOR HELP.

DAVERKOMICS.COM

ALLISON COLE

HAS CONTRIBUTED TO MANY ANTHOLOGIES INCLUDING STUDYGROUP 12, BLOOD ORANGE, AND KRAMERS ERGOT. HER GRAPHIC NOVEL, NEVER ENDING SUMMER, WAS PUBLISHED BY ALTERNATIVE COMICS.

COMICSOFLOVE.COM

SCIENCE FICTION AFFLICTION

RAINA LEE

RECEIVED A B.A. IN SOCIOLOGY FROM UC DAVIS AND A MASTERS IN MEDIA STUDIES FROM THE NEW SCHOOL FOR SOCIAL RESEARCH. SHE IS THE CREATOR OF 1-UP, A VIDEO GAME CULTURE ZINE.

1UP-ZINE.COM

MARK S. DISCHLER

IS THE ARTS EDITOR AND CO-FOUNDER OF THE INDIE PUBLISHING COMPANY NARROW BOOKS. HE IS ALSO THE DESIGNER AND PUBLISHER OF THE WEB MAGAZINE AND ONLINE COMMUNITY A-DICTION.COM

NARROWBOOKS.COM

THE UNHAPPY FUTURE

CHRISTOPHER LEPKOWSKI

IS A WRITER AND CO-FOUNDER OF NARROW BOOKS, A SMALL PRESS IN L.A. ITS FIRST RELEASE, TWO LETTERS, A COLLECTION OF ART AND WRITING, DEBUTED IN 2005.

NARROWBOOKS.COM

JAMES MC SHANE

CREATES TINY TREASURES. HIS SMALL BUT THICK MINIS HAVE BEEN PRAISED IN MANY ONLINE REVIEWS, ARTICLES AND BLOGS. HIS COMICS INCLUDE <u>CARMINE AND DARNEL AND THE SLEEPY CREATURES</u>, AND <u>FIX AND OTHER STORIES</u>.

HEPILOPTER.NET

RON REGÉ, JR.

HAS APPEARED IN <u>KRAMERS ERGOT</u>, <u>MCSWEENY'S</u> AND <u>THE NEW GRAPHICS REVIVAL</u>. HE CREATED A SERIES OF STRIPS AND LIMITED EDITION TOYS FOR TYLENOL'S OUCH! CAMPAIGN. HIS BOOK, <u>SKIBBER BEE-BYE</u> WAS RE-PUBLISHED BY DRAWN AND QUARTERLY.

GEOCITIES.COM/RONREGEJR

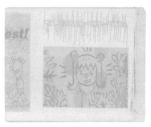

ERIC NAKAMURA

IS THE FOUNDER OF <u>GIANT ROBOT</u>, AN EVER-GROWING SUPPORTER AND FACILITATOR OF THE ZINE WORLD THROUGH ITS MAGAZINE, ART EXHIBITIONS, AND STORES IN NEW YORK, LOS ANGELES AND SAN FRANCISCO.

GIANTROBOT.COM

PAT RIOT

CREATES THOUGHT-PROVOKING WORKS OF ART DISGUISED AS DITTOED PAMPHLETS OF AUTHORITY AND DOUBLETALK. WORKS INCLUDE <u>BUCK WILD</u>, <u>SO...I AM YOUR FATHER</u>, AND <u>THE TAKE OVER TEST</u>. HE ALSO SILKSCREENS HIS OWN PROPAGANDA T-SHIRTS.

POPULAR VULTURE.COM

ANDERS NILSEN

WAS AWARDED THE XERIC GRANT FOR <u>THE BALLAD OF THE TWO-HEADED BOY</u>. HIS COMIC <u>DOGS AND WATER</u> WAS PUBLISHED BY DRAWN AND QUARTERLY. HIS SERIES <u>BIG QUESTIONS</u> WAS NOMINATED FOR THE IGNATZ AWARD.

ANDERSNILSEN.COM

JOE ROCCO

SELF-PUBLISHED HIS ONE PANEL CARTOON, <u>INQUIRING MINDS</u>, FOR 10 YEARS AND ILLUSTRATED THE WEEKLY NATIONALLY SYNDICATED JOE BOB'S AMERICA. HIS WORK HAS APPEARED IN MANY MAGAZINES AND NEWSPAPERS INCLUDING <u>NICKELODEON</u> AND <u>SEATTLE WEEKLY</u>.

SECRETSAUCESTUDIOS.COM

SAELEE OH

CREATES HAND-MADE GOODIES, ZINES, AND CUT-PAPER PAINTINGS. HER WORK HAS BEEN EXHIBITED AT NEW IMAGE ART, SUBLIMINAL PROJECTS, GIANT ROBOT, AND IN MAGAZINES RANGING FROM <u>BUST</u> TO <u>TIME</u>.

SAELEEOH.COM

SOUTHER SALAZAR

OBSESSIVELY DRAWS, MAKES ZINES AND CREATES GALLERY INSTALLATIONS WITH AN EYE FOR DETAIL AND MIXED MEDIA. HIS BOOK, <u>DESTINED FOR DIZZINESS</u>, WAS PUBLISHED BY BUENAVENTURA PRESS. DRAGONFLY, A COLLECTION OF HIS WORK, WAS RELEASED BY GIANT ROBOT.

SOUTHERSALAZAR.NET

PAPER RAD

IS AN ARTISTS COLLECTIVE. THEY HAVE AN ONLINE SITE THAT EXPLODES WITH CREATIVE INSANITY. TOGETHER THEY MAKE MUSIC, COMICS, VIDEOS, AND EXHIBITIONS THAT REFERENCE POP CULTURE.

PAPERRAD.ORG

BWANA SPOONS

MAKES ART, PUBLISHES ZINES, AND CURATES ART SHOWS. HIS ZINES INCLUDE <u>PENCIL FIGHT</u> AND <u>SOFT SMOOTH BRAIN NOW WITH LOGS</u>. HE IS WORKING ON A SERIES OF TOYS CALLED "MY PEEPLES."

GRASSHUTCORP.COM

JOHN PORCELLINO

STARTED MAKING ZINES IN 1983. HIS SIMPLE, HONEST, AND AUTOBIOGRAPHICAL COMIC, <u>KING-CAT</u>, HAS BEEN HIGHLY REGARDED, INFLUENCING MANY OVER THE YEARS TO BEGIN THEIR OWN ZINES.

KING-CAT.NET

DAN ZETTWOCH

HAS AN ONLINE SHOP WHERE YOU CAN FIND AN ARRAY OF ZINES AND COMICS. HIS WORK HAS APPEARED IN <u>KRAMERS ERGOT</u> AND <u>KITCHEN SINK</u>, AND HE SELF-PUBLISHES AN ONGOING COMIC CALLED <u>REDBIRD</u>.

USSCATASTROPHE.COM

HOW I MAKE MY ZINE by DAVE KIERSH

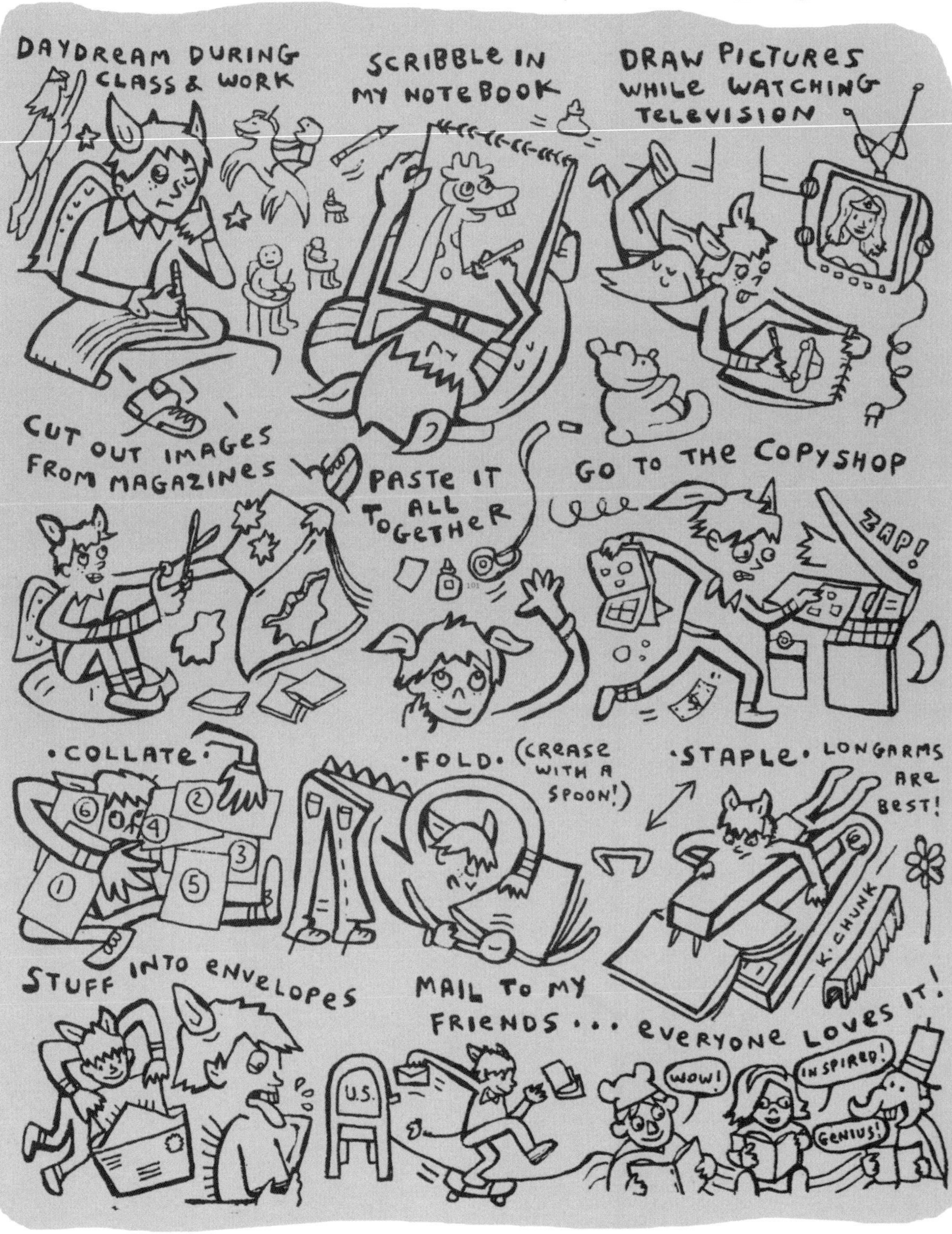
DAYDREAM DURING CLASS & WORK
SCRIBBLE IN MY NOTEBOOK
DRAW PICTURES WHILE WATCHING TELEVISION
CUT OUT IMAGES FROM MAGAZINES
PASTE IT ALL TOGETHER
GO TO THE COPYSHOP
ZAP!
•COLLATE•
1
2
3
4
5
6
•FOLD• (CREASE WITH A SPOON!)
•STAPLE• LONGARMS ARE BEST!
K-CHUNK
STUFF INTO ENVELOPES
MAIL TO MY FRIENDS ... EVERYONE LOVES IT!
U.S.
WOW!
INSPIRED!
GENIUS!

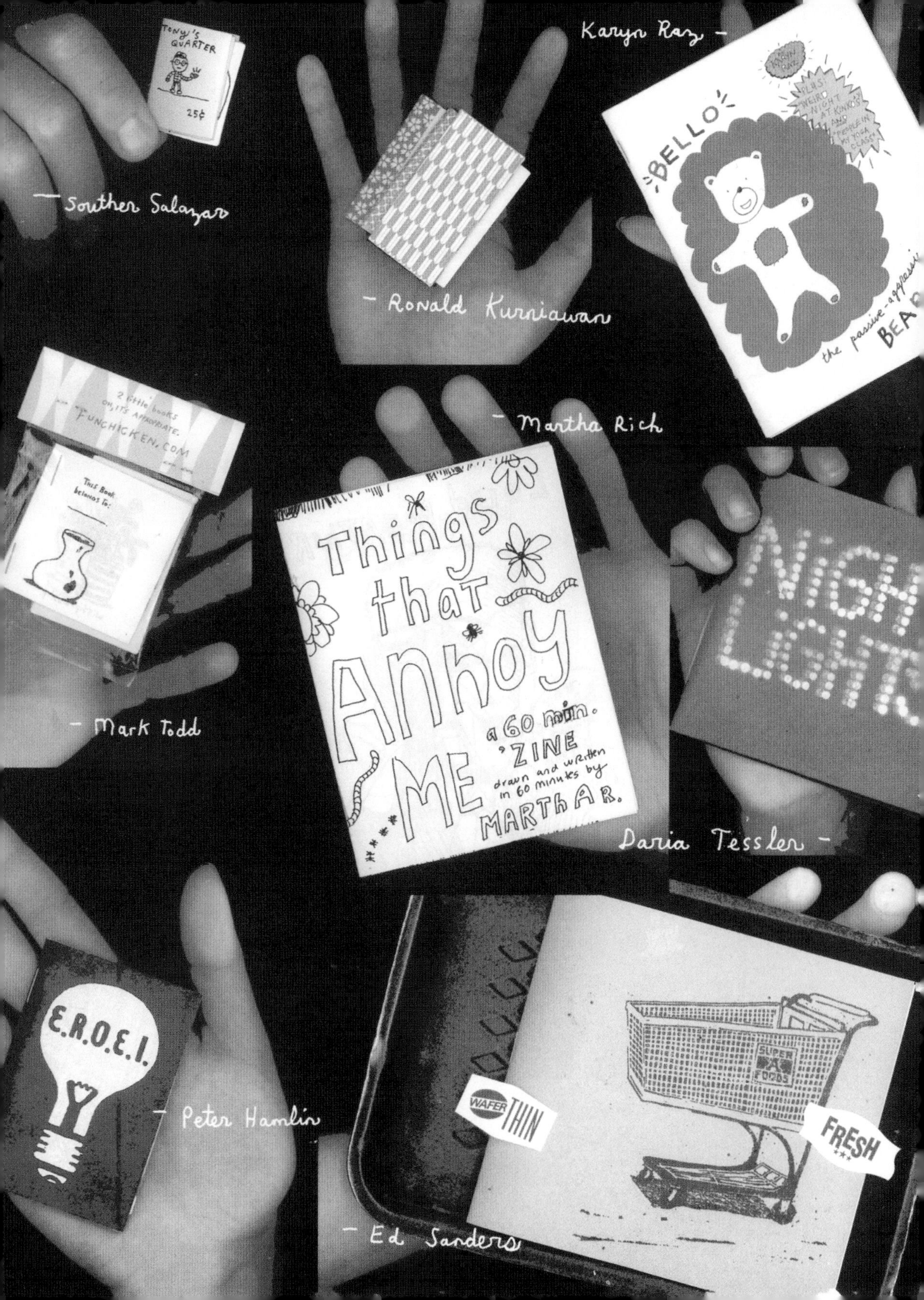

TONY'S QUARTER
25¢
— Souther Salazar
Karyn Raz —
BELLO
PLUS: WEIRD NIGHT AT KINKO'S AND "PEOPLE IN MY YOGA CLASS"
— Ronald Kurniawan
— Martha Rich
FUNCHICKEN.COM
This Book belongs to:
Things that Annoy ME
a 60 min. 'ZINE drawn and written in 60 minutes by MARThA R.
— Mark Todd
Daria Tessler —
E.R.O.E.I.
— Peter Hamlin
WAFER THIN
FRESH
— Ed Sanders

⟨START.⟩